STRANGE JOURNEY

Maud Cairnes

BRITISH LIBRARY

First published in 1935

This edition published in 2022 by
The British Library
96 Euston Road
London NW1 2DB

Cataloguing in Publication Data
A catalogue record for this publication is available from the British Library

ISBN 978 0 7123 5495 0
e-ISBN 978 0 7123 6764 6

Text design and typesetting by JCS Publishing Services Ltd
Printed and bound by CPI Group (UK), Croydon, CR0 4YY

CONTENTS

~

~ ~ ~

THE 1930s

~

~ The 1930s is the decade during which films with sound, commonly known as 'talkies', overtake silent films. The transition is not immediate – the first talkie is released in 1927, and silent films continue to be made throughout the 1930s, but the 'silent era' is widely considered to be over.

~ **1931:** The census shows there are 1.3 million women and 78,489 men employed as indoor domestic staff.

~ **1931:** There are 3,764 divorces in the UK.

~ **1933 (July):** Sheila Borrett becomes the first female radio announcer on the BBC. She is removed from the position in November that year, after the BBC receive thousands of complaints.

~ **1935:** *Strange Journey* is published.

~ **1935:** 711,426 babies are born in the UK. The average number of children that UK women would have throughout their life is 1.79 – down from 4.86 a century earlier.

~ **1935:** A Rolls-Royce 'Phantom III' costs upwards of £1,850.

~ **1935:** The UK national average salary, across all sectors, is £150.

～ ～ ～

～ The number of women who smoke rises significantly during the 1930s. By the end of the decade, women smoke 500 cigarettes a year on average.

~ ~ ~

MAUD CAIRNES (1893-1965)

~

Maud Cairnes was born in 1893, the eldest child of Warner Hastings, 15th Earl of Huntingdon, and Maud, Countess of Huntingdon. Her full name was Lady Maud Kathleen Cairnes Plantagenet Hastings, from which she took two names to publish her works of fiction, though she was known as Lady Kathleen.

In 1916, Lady Kathleen married William Montagu Curzon-Herrick, the son of soldier and Conservative politician Colonel Hon. Montagu Curzon. They lived at Beaumanor Hall near Loughborough, in Leicestershire, which Lady Kathleen's husband had inherited the previous year. The couple held frequent house parties, including those dedicated to shooting, and in 1923 Beaumanor Hall would host the wedding between Lady Kathleen's cousin and Queen Mary's nephew, Lord Eltham. In 1939, the estate was requisitioned by the War Office and became a secret listening station, intercepting encrypted enemy signals and sending them to Bletchley Park for decoding.

Lady Kathleen was keenly interested in culture, and frequently went to the ballet and enjoyed concerts and plays – her own play *It is Expedient* was performed at the Lyceum's Stage Club in the 1920s. *Strange Journey* was her first novel, published in 1935 to very positive reviews. The noted critic Cyril Connolly called it 'an original and charming story', while the reviewer in *The Spectator* called it 'a remarkable little book: a good novel on a theme that is pure housemaid's delight'. Despite its initial acclaim, *Strange Journey* seems to have been largely forgotten until it was rediscovered and discussed by Brad Bigelow on his Neglected Books site.

Only one further novel appeared under Maud Cairnes' name, 1939's *The Disappearing Duchess*, about a duchess who goes missing from a French villa. She wrote at least one more, *A Story for the Train*, which remains unpublished. After her husband's death in 1945, much of the Beaumanor estate had to be sold to pay death duties. Lady Kathleen died in 1965, at the age of 71.

~ ~ ~

PREFACE

~

Can there be a stranger journey than coming round and finding yourself in an unfamiliar body? *Strange Journey*, by Maud Cairnes, follows the long tradition of the body-swapping story first seen in 1882 with *Vice Versa* by Thomas Anstey Guthrie (writing as F. Anstey). These stories tend to fall into two categories. Either they are funny with only mild peril involved like *Freaky Friday* by Mary Rodgers (1972), or they have an element of horror and terror like *The Victorian Chaise-Longue* by Marghanita Laski (1953) or stories by Arthur Conan Doyle and H.P. Lovecraft. Both categories share the same element of the fantastic. *Strange Journey* falls squarely into the comedic category. However, this gentle story also features a sharp wit and an engaging commentary on both the expectations placed on the protagonists as wives and mothers and the class divide.

There cannot be many of us who have not dreamed of a different life, or even a different body. The story of Lady Elizabeth and Polly Wilkinson shows the consequences of an idle wish. A magic beyond their control upends lives and preconceptions. It is perhaps apt that the original dust jacket for *Strange Journey* depicts the protagonists as puppets dancing to some unknown tune. *Strange Journey* forces the reader to consider how others would view their life if they were suddenly dropped into living it.

~ ~ ~

In light of the subject matter of this novel, it is fascinating to discover that Maud Cairnes' full name was actually Lady Maud Kathleen Cairnes Plantagenet Hastings Curzon-Herrick. An aristocratic woman, she would have been at home in the world of Lady Elizabeth. What highlights Cairnes' skill as a writer is how she expresses the mind and speech of Polly, the middle-class woman on the other side of the body swap. Although this story is light and humorous, it is not just a 'pure housemaid's delight', as an early review describes it. Cairnes deftly weaves together the two lives of Elizabeth and Polly. The narrative neatness does not undermine what the novel tells us about class and society in the 1930s.

Lucy Evans
Curator, Printed Heritage Collections
British Library

~ ~ ~

PUBLISHER'S NOTE

~

The original novels reprinted in the British Library Women Writers series were written and published in a period ranging, for the most part, from the 1910s to the 1950s. There are many elements of these stories which continue to entertain modern readers, however in some cases there are also uses of language, instances of stereotyping and some attitudes expressed by narrators or characters which may not be endorsed by the publishing standards of today. We acknowledge therefore that some elements in the stories selected for reprinting may continue to make uncomfortable reading for some of our audience. With this series, British Library Publishing aims to offer a new readership a chance to read some of the rare books of the British Library's collections in an affordable paperback format, to enjoy their merits and to look back into the world of the twentieth century as portrayed by their writers. It is not possible to separate these stories from the history of their writing and as such the following novel is presented as it was originally published with minor edits only, made for consistency of style and sense. We welcome feedback from our readers, which can be sent to the following address:

British Library Publishing
The British Library
96 Euston Road
London, NW1 2DB
United Kingdom

STRANGE JOURNEY

I

❧

Late on a certain afternoon in September, I was leaning on our front gate contemplating Barling Road.

That sounds romantic, as if I were the heroine of a novel, but it was not romantic really.

I had come out to get a breath of air before Tom got back from the office. I was tired from hard work, because our new maid, Gladys, had not yet arrived, and cross, because there was a marvellous Ronald Colman picture at the Pavilion to which I knew I should not be able to go. In our suburb we get the big pictures quite soon. Ronald Colman is one of my pet film stars. I never know which one is absolutely my favourite; but always prefer the tall dark ones with good features and nice slim figures.

Tom is inclined to be sniffy about romantic films, he prefers the ones that make him laugh. I like a good laugh too but, all the same, do get a thrill from watching a picture with a handsome hero!

This does not mean that I do not find my husband attractive. I could wish that he were a little taller, his hair of a nicer shade (he calls it potato-coloured himself), but I love his round face, with the nose that turns up a little and his round blue eyes that can twinkle so. If it came to a decision, I am sure that I would not alter him the least little bit; still that does not prevent one from realising that good-looking men do exist, especially on the films.

It was a muggy, heavy, sort of evening, with just a touch of damp in the air, and I felt rather gloomy as I looked at the road, thinking of nothing in particular, realising only that my muscles ached.

The road was up for some little way, and a sort of devastated area, consisting of mounds of earth, ropes, poles, and barrels of tar, held up the traffic.

There is not usually much traffic down our way. Barling Road, where we live, is not on what they call a "main route" but, on that evening, there were two lorries which had to manoeuvre in order to pass each other and, in the process, they kept a big car waiting.

It was a grand looking car, low and long, and dark blue, a Rolls Royce, as I know now. Looking at it in the concentrated way in which one gazes at an object when one is too tired to move one's eyes elsewhere, I became aware of a woman seated inside.

Suddenly I felt a longing to change places with her, to get into that big, comfortable looking car, lean back in the soft cushions I felt sure that it contained, while the chauffeur made it glide away through the dusk to some pleasant house where there would be efficient servants and tea waiting, with a silver teapot, thin china, and perhaps hot scones, nice deep arm chairs to sit in, and magazines lying on the table.

This does not mean that I was dissatisfied with life. In all the seven years since my marriage I have never been sorry or regretful once, and that, judging by the daily newspapers with their dozens of mentions of divorce cases, must be a record.

I was twenty-one when I married Tom, seven years ago; he was four years older than I, and making £200 a year. His Aunt Abigail thought we were mad to begin life on that, "in these days," but, what the newspapers call "subsequent events" have proved her wrong.

We have had our ups and downs of course, and my poor Tommy's nose has been pressed very hard to the grindstone in order to achieve our present position, this house in Barling Road, and a girl to help with the housework.

What Tom missed most, I think, was his Saturday afternoon football;

but a married man, and a father, dare not risk getting hurt in any way that would prevent his going to the office.

I had no very easy time either, till we could afford household help. Two kids keep your hands full; and when my sister Ethel, who used to live with us after Mum and Dad died, married Sydney Gresham, I had a good struggle to keep things going. Tom was always a dear and used to say: "It's been worth it to me, Polly; I only hope it has been to you."

Naturally there is only one answer to that. This, however, is what poor Dad's friend, Mr Marshall, would call digression; because this is not the life history of Tom and Polly Wilkinson, of 19, Barling Road, West Wampton, but an account of the most extraordinary experience that a human being ever had. So extraordinary that I, Mary Wilkinson (known as 'Polly') am obliged to write it, even though I do not know how to write, and though no one may read, even after I am dead, what has poured itself on to paper.

To come back to that September evening. At that moment the lorries extricated themselves, the big car made a sound like a deep purr, and really did glide away.

I shook myself out of my day-dream and went back into the house. It was about a week later that the first queer thing happened.

I was sitting alone after supper, mending some of the children's things. Tom was out, because the office staff were giving a dinner to Mr Biggleswade on his retirement.

I put down my sewing and looked at the clock on the mantelpiece. Five minutes to ten. I hoped that Tom would not be very much later, and picked up *Home Chat*.

Turning over the pages, I saw the picture of a car coming along a street at dusk. At once the memory of the car I had watched a week ago flashed into my mind, the scene in the picture was so like the real one, as it had been, that I looked at it for some moments. The longing I had felt to get aboard that Rolls Royce came back to me too. Then, for no reason that I could discover, I felt suddenly dizzy, the whole room seemed to be whirling round me. I shut my eyes. The giddiness had made me bend my head forward. When it passed away I opened my eyes gingerly, and stared—

I was looking down at my hands and they were changed!

My hands are small, rather wide, and decidedly pink; but I was looking at hands of the sort that I should have loved to possess, white and slim, with long fingers and shining almond-shaped nails.

I noticed a wedding ring and another with a large square green stone on the left hand, and another green ring on the right. Then I saw that on my knees was lying a piece of tapestry work, all in different coloured silks; the design was queer and stiff, I thought. My knees were covered with green velvet, which was my dress.

Thinking of course that I must be dreaming, I looked up.

I was sitting in a rather high armchair near a fire, in a room with walls panelled in some light coloured wood. On the walls were pictures of men and women in fancy dress, and there was a picture of a battle over the fireplace, with soldiers wearing powdered wigs.

On a sofa, at the other side of the fire, sat an oldish white-haired lady; she was dressed in black, and was busy knitting.

Two dogs, a big yellow one and a little Cairn terrier, were lying asleep in front of the fire. I thought the room very pleasing to look at. It seemed a little bare, but restful.

A door somewhere behind us opened, and a butler and a footman came in with a tray of jugs and glasses.

The dogs got up and yawned and stretched. The butler went up to the oldish lady and said, "Hot water, madam." "Thank you, Burke." He gave it to her on a little silver tray. Then he came to me. "Barley water, my lady?" I answered, "No, thank you," because barley water always makes me think of influenza.

My voice sounded strange. They say that to hear the true sound of your own voice is impossible, but I knew that mine was coming out quite differently to what it usually does.

The men left the room, leaving the bottles and jugs on the table, and the dogs went with them. The old lady smiled at me and said, "How's the chair getting on?"

I started at the sound of her voice, though it was a nice friendly one, and I could not think what she meant, though I know now that she was alluding to the tapestry work. I merely answered vaguely, "I don't know."

She laughed softly and delightfully, and said, "Well, you haven't been doing much to it for the last ten minutes, have you? Feeling sleepy?"

I sat up straight. "No, perhaps not."

Suddenly I saw my feet, lovely slim feet in a beautiful pair of shoes, and expensive looking silk stockings. I could not help staring admiringly at them. The old lady seemed surprised. She asked, "What's the matter, Elizabeth?"

"Oh—nothing. I was just looking at my stockings."

"Why? Have they got ladders in them?"

"Oh, no—I was just thinking what nice ones they were."

She laughed again.

The door opened then and the dogs came in and ran towards us.

I have always liked dogs. We have not got one, because there has never seemed to be time enough to look after one properly since the children came; and maids never seem to like them, and, as servants are so difficult to get nowadays, one has to study their feelings a great deal; but I have longed for a dog for ages.

I stooped down to pat the Cairn. "What a dear little dog."

As I was about to touch him, he looked up at me, his coat stood up all along his back like a shaving brush, his ears went back and he growled.

"Oh, naughty," I said.

"That's funny," said the old lady, as if she was startled.

"What's the matter with you, Hamish?"

The little dog went backwards, still growling deep in his throat, then he crouched at her feet and began to whine. The big dog then began to think that there was something wrong, his hackles stood up and he joined in the duet of growls.

I said, "They don't seem to like me, which is queer because I am very fond of dogs."

"Are you really, dear?" said the old lady smiling, as though I had made a joke. "I am glad you told me that, but what on earth is the matter with the creatures?"

They were both quite close to her, crouching against her skirt, growling as they looked at me, and then Hamish lifted his head and howled.

"Good Lord, one would think they were seeing ghosts."

She was not smiling now.

I felt scared, the dream was turning into a nightmare. The strange room, the woman I did not know, yet who seemed to know me, the hostile and frightened dogs. I longed to wake up and be at home among my own things.

My heart began to beat violently. I turned giddy again, shut my eyes and clutched the arms of the chair. Everything seemed to whirl.

When the swimmy feeling stopped and I opened my eyes, I saw the landing of the top passage in my own house. I "came to" standing outside the children's door, nearly fell down from shock, and only saved myself by clutching at the rail of the banisters.

How on earth had I got there? I must have been sleep-walking!

My knees were shaking, and there were shivers down my spine.

Carefully I opened the children's door—not a sound; evidently I had not disturbed them.

I shut the door quietly and went downstairs. The sitting room was just as I had left it. I looked at the clock—a quarter past ten—for twenty minutes then I had been dreaming!

I heard Tom's latchkey in the front door, and thanked Heaven that he was home.

– 8 –

I did not tell Tom anything about my strange dream, though I often thought, shudderingly, about it. It was the sleep-walking part which frightened me most; for twenty minutes I had been dreaming vividly, and during that time I had moved about my house without the slightest remembrance of so doing. Anything might have happened, and I should not have known.

However, as days passed and nothing more of that nature occurred and I slept well at night, I stopped worrying about it, and was even beginning to think that I might have imagined the whole thing,—when the next odd event took place. September was very nearly over, but the days were still fairly warm; on one particular afternoon I had got very hot while giving tea to Tom's Aunt Abigail and Cousin Fanny.

Aunt Abigail's visits were always trying, as she was a real one to find fault. Luckily Ethel took the children over to her place for the afternoon. That made me easier in my mind, because I felt sure that if they were present at tea, they would be bound to upset Aunt Abigail somehow, or she them, and also I wanted Gladys quite undistracted, so that she would serve tea in a way that the old girls would think adequate to the occasion.

We had tea at four. Aunt Abigail was as tiresome as usual. She asked where I bought my tea and how much I paid for it, and pronounced that it was too expensive for the quality. She sniffed at the Madeira cake from Pinner's and said that she always preferred "home-made." (I thought that if she knew Gladys' "home-made" she would not). Cousin Fanny failed to find a chair out of the draught, and complained that the bread and butter was cut too thickly, which meant that I had to send for some more; she did not like that because it crumbled, so I had to persuade Gladys to make toast. Then Aunt Abigail disliked the butter.

Gladys got sniffy because I had to keep on ringing and Aunt Abigail found a good deal that was bitter to say about the ways of present-day servants.

Cousin Fanny declared that the manners of the servants in a house always reflected those of its mistress, and deplored the fact that so many people nowadays had no power to make themselves respected.

Aunt Abigail then complained that she never saw Tom nowadays, though she had practically brought him up (which is not true, for I know what Tom thought of her when he was a kiddy). And though I tried my best to explain that he never left the office until six, and then took half-an-hour to get home, she only sniffed and reminded me that there were Saturdays and Sundays.

Altogether I could not consider the party a success especially as, after the departure of the guests, Gladys relieved her feelings by smashing two cups and a milk jug, and giving notice when I blew her up. I only pacified her after much trouble.

When I was at last able to sit down and breathe quietly for a moment, my thoughts turned longingly towards the two men-servants of my dream, with their quiet movements and respectful manners. I was thinking of that dream house, and how lovely it would have been to ask Aunt Abigail to tea there when I went dizzy again and was obliged to shut my eyes.

I nearly fell down when I opened them, because I found myself not sitting, as I had thought, but walking—out of doors. In my hand was a stick and my feet were in strong shoes (though somehow they did not look clumsy). I looked round and discovered that I was on a drive, with trees each side of it and a park all round. Cows were walking about loose, with no fence between them and myself, which was alarming. I consoled myself by thinking that, as this *was* a dream, if one of them were to toss me, I should be sure to wake up.

The big yellow dog, Brandon, was trotting along beside me, while Hamish scuttled away in front, which made me tremble with fear that he might chase the cows. I believed them to be only dream cows—but still—"Hamish," I called.

He came back, wagging his tail, and then, exactly as he had done on that other night, he laid back his ears and growled. Brandon, who had come to see what the matter was, behaved in the same way. I felt, rather irritably, how absurd it was that, being perfectly able to make friends with dogs in real life, I should be unable to do so in a dream! I spoke to them and tried to pat them, but they shivered and shrank from me. At last Hamish howled and rushed off with his tail between his legs, while Brandon, still growling, kept as far away from me as he could.

Eventually I gave up trying to conciliate them, and simply walked on, looking at the scenery, admiring the lovely red, gold and brown of the trees, and not omitting to appreciate the attractive tweed of my coat and skirt.

I was disturbed in my contemplation by the sound of a car coming up behind me. I moved aside to let it pass, but it stopped a few yards ahead of where I was, and a fat short woman bounced out of it and bustled up to me, holding out her hands.

She gushed, "Dear Lady Elizabeth, what luck, I had *so* hoped to find you in!"

It appeared to me (if I was Lady Elizabeth) that at present I was out of doors, but I smiled vaguely, and said, "How do you do?" as she energetically shook my hand.

She continued speaking, "I've brought Hilda Burslem over, she is staying with me and is dying to see Heringdon."

I could think of nothing to answer her but "Oh."

"Do let's give you a lift back."

She bustled me into the car, where we found a lanky woman with a thin white face and very red lips.

"You don't know Mrs Burslem?"

I smiled, still rather vaguely, at the thin woman, who smiled back, murmuring some politeness which I did not catch.

"What about your dog?" asked the fat one.

Brandon was standing by the roadside looking very fierce.

"Oh, please don't worry about him," said I.

The door was shut and the car started. We all three sat on the back seat. Mrs Burslem spoke in a drawling voice: "I hear, Lady Elizabeth, that you have some wonderful examples of stump work."

Startled, I put my hand up to my mouth.

"I've only got one stump, and that's crowned," was what I was about to say, when she went on:

"I adore Restoration things, don't you?"

I thought that all this enthusiasm about teeth seemed odd, but before I could think of anything to say, the fat lady suddenly called out, "Oh, there's Mrs Forrester. Is she staying with you now?" She pressed a button, the car stopped, and I saw, walking on the drive, the white-haired old lady of my dream, dressed in very nice out-of-door clothes. The fat lady opened the door and got out.

"Dear Mrs Forrester, we've just picked up Lady Elizabeth."

Mrs Forrester looked rather worried, I thought, as she came to the door of the car, asking: "Is anything the matter? Hamish has just come back to the house, looking frightened to death."

As she was obviously expecting an answer, I felt obliged to say something.

"He howled and ran away," I volunteered.

She did not seem comforted, "How very odd."

Mrs Burslem then drawled, "Perhaps he saw a ghost. Nina always thinks that animals are psychic."

"I am sure of it," said the fat lady; "they have a faculty which we have lost."

As there was a silence after this pronouncement, 'Nina' took charge. Somehow she packed us all into the car, and we went on until we arrived at the front door of a large house, where we all disembarked.

Mrs Burslem stayed gazing at the house.

"Too marvellous—Charles II, is it not?"

As I did not know, I said nothing.

"Partly Charles II, partly Queen Anne, some bits earlier," said Mrs Forrester.

To me the house looked very big, parts of it reminded me of Hampton Court. We stood on the gravel, staring for a little while, and Mrs Forrester looked at me as if she expected me to do something. Then she said.

"Well, shall we go in?" and opened the front door.

We found ourselves in a hall full of furniture. Mrs Burslem enthused, and 'Nina' also had a good deal to say.

Then somehow we drifted into another room, with red silk brocade on the walls and several pictures, but what I chiefly noticed were flowers in quantities.

I love flowers, but can never have as many as I should like because, once summer is over, the more thrilling kinds get so expensive, even though bought off the barrows in the street.

I was gazing hard at a beautiful vase full, when I heard Mrs Burslem murmur at my elbow, "Never have I seen a more perfect Lely."

"Lily? It's a dahlia," I cried indignantly, thinking that at least, in the vase in front of me, was something I *did* know all about.

"I meant the picture," said Mrs Burslem coldly, and I could only say "Oh" again.

The butler and two footmen had been coming in and out of the room during all this time preparing tea. It was the sort of tea I had always longed to have. A silver kettle hung over a flame, there was a silver teapot, jug, and so on, pretty, thin china, and masses of glorious things to eat.

Having had no tea to speak of at home, owing to the bother with Aunt Abigail and Cousin Fanny, I hoped that these people would soon think of beginning.

There was a pause as if everybody was waiting for something, and then Mrs Forrester said: "Well, Elizabeth, what about giving us some tea?"

So I was the hostess. This was my house. Mrs Forrester, I supposed, was a visitor. The other two, Mrs Burslem, and 'Nina,' whose other name I had discovered to be Mrs Hempson, were obviously callers.

While I was making the tea they all talked, especially Mrs Hempson, mentioning all sorts of names of people and places about which I knew nothing. I thought that strange, because in dreams, as a rule, you dream about things you *have* heard of.

I thought Mrs Hempson rather rude, as she ate all sorts of things before they had been offered to her, so I asked Mrs Burslem, who had politely waited, to have something.

She answered, "Thanks, but I never touch tea."

"Like you, Elizabeth," said Mrs Forrester.

"Oh, is it," I thought. Dream or no dream, I was not going to miss a tea like that. Not likely. I was a little afraid that the glorious looking food might taste horrible, as food in dreams generally does, but it did not and I had a very good tuck in, though I would have been more comfortable if I could have been sitting up at a proper dining-room table.

There were little hot scones in covered plates, so light that they melted in one's mouth, with large dabs of butter in them, ever so many sorts of sandwiches, some made with white bread and some with brown, cut very thin, all with marvellous flavours, plates of different kinds of little cakes, some of them with cream inside, and big cakes too. I wondered if a party had been expected, but I could only see four cups.

"Are you expecting Major Forrester back to-day?" asked Mrs Hempson.

"I don't know," was all that I could truthfully answer, and thought that they all looked surprised.

Shortly afterwards 'Nina' said, "I suppose we must be going, but might Hilda have just a peep at more of your divine rooms?"

"Oh, please, I should adore that," said the other caller. "Nina has told me such a lot about your marvellous Heringdon."

We all went and looked at ever so many more rooms. Mrs Burslem admired hard, and got very excited over some dingy looking beady boxes and baskets, and told me that she collected stump work too.

We went upstairs and into a long gallery. Mrs Forrester had done all the explaining; she had looked at me several times as though expecting me to help, but naturally I could not.

I began to get tired of looking at things, museums have never interested me very much, and hoped that the callers would soon go; but, just as I saw hope of going downstairs again, Mrs Hempson asked:

"May we just have a peep at your room, Lady Elizabeth? I should love Hilda to see that glorious bed."

It seemed to me odd that even in a dream I should not know the way to my own bedroom, but I did not; and the tour of inspection followed Mrs Forrester into a grand room, with a very big four-poster bed, covered in a greeny-bluish looking stuff that seemed to excite Mrs Burslem wildly. I strolled over to the dressing table, which was a very big one. There was a triple mirror on it and any amount of things. Brushes, and a hand glass, all made of thick tortoiseshell with squirly gold monograms on them, lots of boxes of the same material, cut-glass bottles and scent sprays. Instinctively I looked in the glass.

It gives one the most peculiar feeling in the world to see a strange face reflected in a mirror instead of one's own. Of course I had realised that I must be different from my usual self, but not how completely. My round, pinkish, rather freckled face had become pale and oval; in it were big dark blue eyes under long lashes. I was admiring myself so intently that I quite jumped when I heard 'Nina's' voice in my ear, asking if they might just glance at the divine fireplace in Major Forrester's room. Of course I said yes.

It appeared that Major Forrester's room opened out of mine. However, Mrs Forrester seemed quite calm about it.

It made me feel a little shy when we all went into the gentleman's room, even though he was not there. I hoped the dream was not going to turn out improper. Tom says that a German scientist has discovered how, when you dream naughty things, it means that you have all sorts of unpleasant sides to your nature.

However, nothing dreadful happened. We all went downstairs again and 'Nina' asked for her car. I *did* know what to do about that, so I rang the bell and said, "Burke, Mrs Hempson's car," when the butler appeared, just as I had seen Celia Hooper do in the film, *Worried Wives*.

Everybody said "good-bye" soon after that, and Mrs Hempson asked me to lunch next week. I replied that I should love to if I were still here, and when she appeared surprised and said, "Oh, are you going away?" I answered with a smile, "One never knows, does one?" which made her stare.

When they had gone, Mrs Forrester lit a cigarette, saying, "What a visitation," and passed me the box.

"No, thank you." She looked at me rather curiously.

"Are you feeling all right, Elizabeth?"

"Yes, why?"

"You seemed half asleep all the afternoon, and never smoked a cigarette."

I was about to say that smoking made me sick, when she went on:

"You can't be seedy, or you wouldn't have eaten that colossal tea—I've never seen you do that before."

"Teas are made to be eaten." She looked puzzled, opened her mouth as if to say something, changed her mind and shut it again.

At that moment a clock "tinged" somewhere. She started, "Good lord, half-past six, and I've never written to Dora, I had better do it now."

She hurried to a writing table and sat down.

Half-past six, the children's bed time, and I was asleep dreaming! I thought of them waiting in the nursery, wondering what had happened. Then the giddiness that I was beginning to know came over me. I shut my eyes.

When I opened them I found myself in the children's room with Bobby's howls ringing in my ears.

III

The room seemed to sway and spin for a moment or two then it steadied itself. I drew a deep breath and looked about me.

Betty was kneeling up in her cot, leaning on the rail, and Bobby was standing howling on the floor.

"Moggy, Moggy, I want Moggy!"

"Stop that Bobby."

"Mogg*ee*."

"Be quiet, I'll get you Moggy."

I fished from its place in the cupboard the terrible, woolly one-eyed beast, without which Bobby will never go to bed, and gave it to him. He stopped howling.

"Jump into bed at once, Bobby. Fancy a big boy of nearly five and a half crying like that. Aren't you ashamed of yourself?"

"But you wouldn't give me Moggy."

"You've got Moggy now, so don't be silly."

He quietened down and I tucked him up in bed. Both children were in their night clothes, with every appearance of having had their baths. The tray with their milk and biscuits was on the table. I felt sick and frightened.

Had I undressed and bathed them in my sleep?

Perhaps Gladys had done it.

"Come on, Betty, drink up your milk, there's a dear."

She opened her eyes wide, "Tell me the end of the 'tory about the 'tag on the hill."

"The—what?"

"The 'tag wif big horns."

"Yes, in Kirrie Glen," this from Bobby in the other bed, "it's a lovely story."

I could not understand what they were talking about.

"If you are good kiddies, and go to sleep nicely now, I'll tell you about Red Riding Hood to-morrow."

"I like the 'tag better, it's more 'citing," said Betty.

Tom then came in. "I say, Polly, aren't you ever coming! These kids are taking an awful time getting to bed, and what was all that bawling about?"

"Mummy wouldn't give me Moggy," began Bobby.

"You've got Moggy now," said I sternly. "Say night-night to Daddy, and go to sleep like good children."

Tom and I said good-night to them, and saw them settle down; after which I went down to talk over the day with Tom.

He was not extra pleased at being kept waiting, because he wanted to tell me about some trouble they were having in the office, which was worrying him. His preoccupation with that kept him from noticing that I was shaky and upset. As he was bothered himself I did not want to fuss him about anything else, so told him nothing about my adventure.

That night I lay awake for a long time after Tom had gone to sleep, wondering if I were going mad. I had certainly put the children to bed and told them a story about a stag without remembering anything about it, and while feeling exactly as though I had been doing something quite different somewhere else.

Gladys, I discovered, had brought the children's supper and noticed nothing unusual. I found that out by asking her why she had come up to the nursery so late, which she indignantly denied, and wanted to know why I had said nothing about it at the time.

Ethel dropped in next morning, seeming rather huffy about something. She began by saying:

"I hope you've got out of bed the right side to-day, Polly."

"What do you mean, Eth?"

"Well, you were in a very haughty mood yesterday, weren't you? Behaving to me as if you had never set eyes on me before. A nice way to treat your only sister, I must say."

"I didn't mean it," I said quite truthfully.

She went on, "After me taking the children off your hands and all. Not that I mind them—still I did have them to oblige you."

"I know, and I am very grateful. I promise I did not mean to be haughty."

"All right, Polly. Perhaps Abbie and Fanny had put you out a bit. What were they like?"

I told her, and made her giggle. I wondered if I dared tell her the rest of my story but, as she was going to have a baby, I did not want to upset her; besides, she might tell Sydney and he might think that I was crazy, and perhaps try and get Tom to make me see doctors who would want to shut me up away from my family.

I could not bear the thought of that.

Before Ethel left I asked her if she had told the kids any stories. She said, "No."

I went about in terror all that day, dreading an attack of giddiness coming on, but it did not come. I tried my best to think of everyday things, of anything except my dream. It was quite easy to do that, as it happened, for Tom came home that evening still more worried about the trouble at his office, and was even afraid that he might get the sack. That occupied both our minds for several days; but, thank Heaven, everything was put right in the end, largely owing to Tom himself, who managed so well that he was complimented by Mr Bendale, and promised an unexpectedly big rise at Christmas.

We were very happy when that news came. It meant that we would be able to pay off several bills which were rather a bother, and perhaps even afford another girl to help Gladys, which would make things much easier for me. I felt so much better after this happened, that I began to think it must have been only overwork that had made me queer, and that I would not be likely to have any more uncanny experiences.

Once or twice, it is true, I had a curious feeling, as if something were tugging at my brain, but, when it came, I thought as hard as I could of anything ordinary, even recited the multiplication tables to keep my imagination in order.

Time passed. Came the middle of November. I went up to London one afternoon to do some shopping.

There was a special kind of silk I needed for a lining, so I thought I might get it at Harrods', having tried our local shops in vain.

I was sitting at a counter, and the young lady assistant had gone to look for what I wanted, when I heard a voice behind me say, "Why—Mrs Forrester, how are you?"

I jumped in my shoes, and looked round. There, sitting at the opposite counter, was the old lady of my dreams, being talked to by a young smartly dressed woman. I felt my eyes and mouth open, and knew that I was gaping at her. There was such a singing in my ears that I could not hear anything for a moment or two; when it stopped I heard Mrs Forrester say, "Yes, I shall be at Heringdon then."

"Well, give my love to Elizabeth and Gerald."

"Thanks, I certainly will."

The young lady went off. Mrs Forrester got up and came towards me. I could not take my eyes off her. She looked at me as if I were not there, not rudely, but as one glances uninterestedly at a stranger in the street, and passed on while I stared after her.

I heard the voice of my assistant talking about silk, pulled myself together with an effort, and tried to attend to my shopping. I did give one quick glance at my hands but, in their rather tight gloves, they were unchanged.

When I left the shop my knees were shaking. I pinched myself. It hurt. I was not dreaming. I was myself, Polly Wilkinson, quite real, on the way to take the bus home; *but* I had seen Mrs Forrester, who was a character in a dream. Every minute I expected to find myself in those dream surroundings; I could not stop thinking of that house, but nothing happened. I caught my bus and arrived safely home.

It was all I could do to be natural with Tom that evening, and tell him about my afternoon in town. I went to bed early, with a headache. I was quite sure now that I was going mad. One of Tom's friends had an uncle in an asylum. He began by seeing things and people that were not really there—having hallucinations, they called it.

I wondered if my madness was the harmless sort, or if it would turn to mania. That friend of Tom's had told us a great deal about lunatics, and how cunning they were. I determined to be cunning too, and hide the truth as long as I could.

The worst of it was that I began to lose my appetite and look ill. Tom noticed it, and wanted me to see the doctor. I refused with force, as I was afraid that a doctor might find me out; after a week, however, my panic grew less. I was still frightened, but not so violently. I had thought of the dream house a good deal, and nothing had happened, and I began to think that perhaps Mrs Forrester was not an hallucination after all.

Might I not possibly have seen her somewhere, sometime, forgotten and dreamed about her? Might she not really have been in Harrods' that afternoon? Of course, that did not explain my sleep-walking, or the story I had told the children, but people have been known to walk in their sleep, and even talk, without being mad at all.

I suppose that I really am a cheerful person, because I find it difficult to worry about things for long, unless they are very bad indeed; and as the impression on my mind grew fainter I began to think that, perhaps, I had been rather silly. It is true that I could not quite get rid of a feeling that something was waiting to pounce on me. I was braced for a shock.

I got the shock all right, and in the last place where I would have expected to receive it. Some of my teeth wanted stopping, and I had to go to the dentist one day. There were several people in the waiting room, and they had taken all the *Punch's* and *Tatlers*. I did not fancy the *Autocar*, so I took up a copy of *Country Life* and began to turn over the pages. Suddenly I saw the picture of a house. I looked and looked harder,—at the top of the page was written "Heringdon Place, the seat of Major G. S. Forrester, D.S.O."

Carefully, I put down the paper and looked around the room. The people were still there, seemingly quite solid. The *Punch's* were still being read, unsmilingly. I studied *Country Life* again; there was the front of the house exactly as I had seen it. The hall, the yellow drawing-room, the dining-room. I felt sure that my mind could not hallucinate a whole article in *Country Life*, but I thought I would make a test.

I turned to the lady sitting next to me, and spoke:

"Excuse me."

She jerked upright as if I had stuck a pin into her, but I was not discouraged. I went on:

"I can't read print very well without my glasses, could you tell me what is written underneath this picture?"

"Certainly." She took up the paper and read out:

"Heringdon Place. The West Front."

"Thank you very much." She returned the paper to me, saying, "Not at all," and returned her attention to the *Tatler*. I put down the *Country Life* and swallowed hard, because my throat suddenly felt very dry. There was no doubt about it, Heringdon was a real house.

IV

When the dentist had finished with my teeth, I went home a good deal happier than I had been for some time. Extraordinary as the whole situation was, I was now sure that my brain was not cracked. There was a real house called Heringdon, belonging to people called Forrester.

I had heard about trances, and now felt convinced that in a trance state my mind had somehow travelled to that house and enabled me to see things that were happening there, while my subconscious mind carried on with my everyday life at home. It was all rather exciting and I hoped that I should have another trance journey soon.

One thing puzzled me a good deal. The dogs, Brandon and Hamish, had spotted that I was a sort of ghost, while Mrs Forrester and the other people had not seemed in the least surprised to see me, and had talked to me as if they knew me.

I must be very stupid, for the real solution of this mystery was not plain to me until much later. Yet, in defence of my intelligence, I must insist that the experience was an unusual one, and the beginning of it weird enough to make me certain that the whole thing was an illusion.

With the fear of insanity gone from me, I cheered up and got better, which pleased Tom who had been fussing about me. It was not a particularly good time for him to be worried, for Mr Bendale had put a good deal more responsibility than usual on him, and Tom was very anxious to make good. He worked very hard, which made him tired, and of course when people are tired they get snappy, especially husbands, I think.

About the middle of December, Tom had to go to Manchester on special business for the firm, and, though he was glad in a way, as it gave him a chance to show what he could do, he grumbled a good deal because he would not be able to get back in time to see a certain football match on Saturday afternoon to which he had been looking forward for some time.

While he was away, I tried to think of something which would make up to him for missing the match. I did not think he would be inclined to go to the pictures after a long journey, and might be even too tired for a game of bridge with the Simmonses from next door; and just sitting at home with me would hardly seem enough like a treat.

Finally, I asked Bill Jorkins to supper, as it amuses Tom to talk politics with him. I am no good at politics, as I always find them so difficult to be interested in, and they seem to make people so cross, especially when there is a Budget, as something always seems to get more expensive then.

It was just after I had telephoned to Bill on that December Saturday morning, that my mind went off to Heringdon, and I felt the "trance" feeling again. This time I shut my eyes, and waited peacefully for the dizziness to pass. When I opened them I found myself in a room I did not know, sitting at a writing table in front of a window.

I soon saw, as I looked out, that this was an upstairs room. The view was over a big park full of very fine trees; of course they were bare, but I could imagine what it would look like in summer.

There was a letter on the blotter before me, just begun, with the words *Dearest Dora*. I had a pen in one hand and a cigarette in the other. I put down both, one into an ash tray, the other on an ink-stand, then got up and surveyed the room.

It was smaller and somehow cosier than the other rooms I had visited. The walls were panelled in white and there were pictures of flowers hanging on them, rather old-fashioned looking. There was a sofa, covered in faded looking embroidered stuff and some worked chairs. The curtains were of rather faded looking cream and red colour with a pattern, and

I wondered why in such a grand house they did not have newer and smarter looking fabric. At the end of the room was a small grand piano, it looked newer than the other things, but very bare. I wondered why they had not put some ornaments on it, because there were any amount of flowers and books and things on other tables. There was a carpet on the floor that looked more like a big rug than a regular carpet; it did not quite cover the floor and left quite a lot of the boards showing, and though they looked polished they were rather uneven. I should have covered them up. There were bookcases too, with a good many books in them, some in coloured bindings made of leather, and some very old and faded looking; these were mostly in worn brown covers with faint gold lines on them. There were a certain number in paper covers also; these mostly had foreign names written on them. They were not put in neat rows, according to size, as you might have expected, but had an up-and-down appearance.

In front of a well-burning log fire was a thick white mat, and Hamish was asleep on it.

On the writing table was the photograph of an officer in uniform. I picked it up and had a good gaze at it, because his appearance was really most thrilling, more even than that of Ronald Colman. He had a longish face with a straight nose and a firm chin. I thought his mouth looked sarcastic under his dark moustache. He was not exactly handsome, but I felt sure he was attractive, though his expression was stern. I was wondering who he might be when someone knocked at the door. I put the photo hurriedly down on the piano and called out, "Come in."

A woman dressed in white appeared. She was wearing an apron and somehow looked starched. She was carrying an exercise book from which hung a pencil tied to a string.

"Oh—er—good morning," I ventured.

"Good morning, my lady." She handed me the book open.

I took it and saw under the date what looked like miles of writing, all in French, as I had seen on menus at the restaurant where Tom takes me sometimes for a birthday treat.

I guessed that this must be the cook, and wondered what I had better do; did I have to choose dishes out of the list, or what? She was evidently waiting for orders. I looked down the list, and saw one familiar word, *Soles*. I knew what that meant even if *à la* something was a mystery to me.

"Oh—er—are the soles fresh to-day?" I asked.

She jumped as though I had startled her.

"Yes, very nice, my lady."

"Oh, then that's all right."

While I was thinking of what to say next, she enquired:

"Will any of the ladies be in to lunch, my lady?"

How should I know, I thought, but said, "I am not sure."

"Perhaps your ladyship will let me know later."

At that moment the door opened and Mrs Forrester came in.

"Are you busy, Elizabeth?"

"Oh no," I said, rather glad of an interruption to my interview with the starchy one, who was looking very stiff.

"Good morning, Mrs Mellon," said Mrs Forrester.

"Good morning, madam," was the reply.

"Are you ordering us a marvellous dinner, Elizabeth?"

"Look and see," I said, giving her the book. She glanced at it and handed it back to me smiling.

"Mrs Mellon takes care of that, doesn't she?"

Then, to the cook, "I must really compliment you on that soufflé of last night, it was a poem."

Mrs Mellon smiled for the first time, and said, "Thank you, madam."

I wondered whether I ought to say more about the menu, but thought on the whole it would be safer not to.

"Well, Mrs Mellon, I am sure that will be all right." I handed her back the book. She thanked me and went.

It seemed to me an easy way of ordering food, though, of course, I had not the smallest idea what it was going to be like. I thought of the brain cudgelling I suffered at home, trying to think out dishes that Tom would like, that Gladys and I could manage to prepare, and that were not too expensive. There seemed to me to have been a great many courses on that menu.

Mrs Forrester's voice brought me back to Heringdon.

"I came to ask you if you had written to Dora yet."

"Oh," then I remembered the letter. "No—not yet."

"What are you going to say to her?"

"I haven't an idea." That answer was easy.

"Well, I have heard from Colonel Slane, and he tells me the mare's a whistler."

I stared, never having known of a horse that whistled.

"Isn't that rather wonderful?" I queried.

The old lady laughed. "Nothing Dora does is surprising. She'd stick her own mother as soon as look at her."

I sat down, this time really out of my depth of understanding. Mrs Forrester went on without noticing my bewilderment.

"I suppose it would do no harm to see the animal, though?"

"Or hear it. Ought not a horse like that to be in a Circus?"

She seemed amused. "You'd better tell Dora that. At any rate, I've given you the tip. By the way, old Cissie's rheumatism's better, and she's coming out to lunch after all."

"Oh, is she?" I murmured feebly.

"Yes, I told her that the car would be starting at half-past twelve with Leonora and Mrs Darnelton, and that we were walking. You are walking as usual, I suppose?"

"Of course!" I answered firmly.

Time would no doubt show where I was expected to walk.

She went on talking for a bit about what a pity it was that somebody or other had "chucked," and added, "Gerald told me he'd got that Champion man to come over, he says he's a good shot. He always strikes me as a bit of a bounder; still one takes one's neighbours as one finds them, I suppose."

To this I could certainly assent, and soon afterwards she talked of going to finish her letters but, just as she reached the door, she turned and said, "Oh—Elizabeth, have you seen Phyllis this morning?"

I took a chance and said, "No."

"Ah, then she hasn't told you anything."

"Nothing," I said, hoping that it was true.

"H'm. It struck me last night that she might have made up her mind, and I knew that you would be the first one to hear if she had."

"Everyone must make up their own minds sometime," said I, feeling that somehow I had expressed myself ungrammatically.

"Well—" she was evidently following a train of thought, "I wonder, Toby's a very nice boy, but I don't know how Phyllis would stand being hard up. Still she's twenty-seven, it's time she settled down."

"Oh, quite." I wondered if she would tell me any more, which might be helpful if I met 'Phyllis' or 'Toby,' whoever they might be, but she only stood thinking for a few moments, and then pulling herself together, spoke briskly:

"I must be off. We meet in the hall at twelve then?"

"Certainly."

Once more she went towards the door, but stopped short in front of the piano.

"You've moved Gerald's picture."

I felt confused, like I did when Tom caught me once, studying Ronald Colman's photo. I am sure I looked shy. I stammered, "I—I—was only l-l-looking at it. I'll put it back."

I put the frame back on to the writing table and turned towards her. Her expression surprised me. She looked upset, her lips trembled as she spoke, and her voice had dropped several tones lower.

"My dear—you know, I never say anything. Gerald's my son after all—but—I do realise how wonderful you're being."

I was completely bewildered and could think of nothing to say. I felt extremely awkward.

"Damn Leonora," said Mrs Forrester suddenly, with a violence of which I should never have believed her capable, and, before I could answer. "There—I've said it, my dear, and feel better." Thereupon she left the room.

V

⁓

I sat down in an armchair to think, and decided that I must straighten things out in my mind, or I should put my foot in it badly. To begin with, taking the things of which I was sure, Gerald was the name of the man in the photograph; he was Mrs Forrester's son, and *Country Life* had said that Heringdon Place belonged to Major G. S. Forrester. Very good. Then, where did I come in? I was called 'Lady Elizabeth.' The cook came to me for orders, I poured out the tea, but if I was Lady Somebody, I could not be Major Forrester's wife, or could I? I could not very well be Mrs Forrester's daughter, and hostess in her house. It was all very puzzling.

Just then Hamish woke up with a start. He shook himself, got up and stretched, then, when he saw me, his ears went back. I determined to put an end to that sort of thing, went to him, spoke to him as if he had been a human being, explaining how much I liked dogs, that I was a kind and gentle person in my real life, and could be no nastier in a trance.

At last he allowed me to stroke him, though his eyes had a wistful expression, and he shivered a good deal.

So busy was I making friends with Hamish, that I did not notice the arrival of someone else into the room, until a voice said: "Hallo! What's wrong with Hamish?"

I scrambled to my feet and saw a pretty girl looking at me; she had a cigarette in a long holder in her mouth.

"Oh—he's had a bad dream, I think," said I, wondering if this could be 'Leonora.'

"Do you maltreat dogs in secret, like the 'Man with Red Hair?'" she asked, smiling. Then she held a book out to me. "I've brought you this back."

"Oh, thanks."

The book was called *Garbage and Carrion*, by Mark Sword.

"He's gone off rather, don't you think?" she asked.

"Sounds like it," I replied, looking at the title.

She went on criticising the book which, I soon gathered, was poetry. As I had never heard of Mark Sword or any of his writings, I answered rather vaguely; she must have grasped this, for soon she said:

"But no doubt I'm disturbing you—if you've got things to do, and all that?"

"Not at all," I assured her.

She hesitated a moment, then spoke: "Eliza—I'd rather like to know what you think—Toby's getting very restive."

I decided that this must be Phyllis.

She looked at me as though she expected me to say something. I played for safety.

"What do you feel about it?" I asked.

She plumped herself down on a sofa and lit another cigarette. "Oh, well—I suppose I'm fond of him all right, he attracts me physically and all that."

I was shocked. People said things like that in books and plays, but it did not seem quite nice in real life, and coming from an unmarried girl. I made some sort of noise in my throat, which might mean anything.

She continued thoughtfully: "In time, of course, he might end by boring me, though I can't imagine it now." Again she looked at me.

I cleared my throat. "My dear Phyllis …" A moment's pause.

"Well, Eliza …?"

I stifled a sigh of relief, she *was* Phyllis.

"Well, Phyllis, it only seems to me that you should make quite sure whether you—er, whether he—er, whether you are both really fond enough of one another. That's the main thing, isn't it?"

"Um—what about the great cash question? I shall never have more than my £200 a year, and he's only got £400 of his own besides what he gets from Snuffy."

I put on a judicial expression.

"£400 saved up is not too bad for a start," I began.

She broke in. "Saved up! You must be potty, darling. How can Toby save, out of £400 a year? Old Snuffy only pays him £500 at present. Perhaps he'll cough up more some day, but Toby isn't the money-making sort. So all we can count on, with combined resources, is £1,100 now."

"A year!" I gasped.

"Yes, it's pretty bloody, isn't it?" She dabbed her cigarette fiercely into the ash-tray.

I stared at her. "You don't think over a thousand a year enough to live on? Millions of people would regard it as a fortune!"

"Oh, don't rag, Eliza, I'm serious."

"So am I." There was no lie about that. In our most optimistic days Tom and I had never dreamed of having an income as big as that.

"Do you really think we could manage on it?"

"Manage. Good heavens, yes! and think yourselves lucky—why—"

"How long would it last you and Gerald, I wonder? A month?" Her voice was sarcastic.

"A m…" I could not speak. Did people really spend sums like that! This Phyllis girl did not seem to be joking. She got up. "Well, if all you can do is to pull my leg, I'll be off."

"No—wait. Phyllis, I wasn't thinking,—I mean—"

She sat down again.

"You mean that Toby and I could live on £1,100." She smiled scornfully.

I felt sorry for her, and spoke very seriously. "People do manage to live happily on a great deal less."

"Um, but it would mean never going anywhere, no decent clothes—and supposing we had a child?"

I smiled.

"England would be very empty if only people with a thousand a year had children."

"Then you think love in a cottage would be a possibility for us?"

"What does Toby think, Phyllis?"

"Oh, he's all for risking it, but I wonder how he'd feel later on. When he found out about all the things he'd have to give up, and saw me looking a frump! When that happens there are always people like Leonora about—" She stopped and looked a little confused.

"What's Leonora got to do with it?" I enquired, genuinely curious to know. She flushed a little.

"Oh, I didn't mean her particularly, but when a woman gets shabby, a man soon finds someone else better turned out to look at. You can't blame him."

"I think you are talking nonsense," said I. "And I truly think that unless you and your Toby believe that all sorts of quite unnecessary things are important, you can't be so utterly different from the rest of the world that it is impossible for you to be happy together unless you are far richer than most people in England ever dream of being."

Her mouth opened and her eyes got round.

"You are queer this morning, Liz. I came to you for a dose of hard common sense, and you are talking like a sentimental novel."

"I can only tell you what I believe to be true."

"And you wouldn't think us mad if we married?"

"If you care for each other, I should think you mad if you didn't."

She laughed. "The family would hardly agree with you. Still—it hasn't happened yet."

"How I wish I could help you—" I meant it.

She half smiled, rather sadly, at me. "You queer creature, who would

– 34 –

ever dream that you hid a romantic heart under that aloof manner of yours. Well, I'll think over your advice, and weigh it. Now I must trot off. Twelve o'clock start isn't it? Meet in the hall, I suppose?"

"I expect so."

She left me.

Start where? I wondered; but I should know in time. I felt as though I had been playing a game of which I had to learn the rules as I went along, without betraying my ignorance to the other players. I really had been sincere with Phyllis, but had I done right?

These people talked a strange language. Eleven hundred a year counted as poverty. Whistling horses! And who was Leonora, why did Mrs Forrester hate her, and Phyllis seem so uncomfortable when her name slipped into the conversation? If they did not like her, why was she staying in the house? She could not be trying to marry Gerald, because he was Lady Elizabeth's husband, at least that was what Phyllis had implied, and I was—temporarily, Lady Elizabeth.

I had another look at that photograph. He did look attractive.

The whole adventure still seemed so dream-like that the thought of Gerald being my husband did not embarrass me at all. I was mainly concerned with minor points of behaviour, such as what I was to call Mrs Forrester; 'Mother,' perhaps, if she was my mother-in-law. At this juncture the lady herself appeared.

"Elizabeth dear—aren't you ready?—it's after twelve—"

She was dressed for going out and carried a shooting stick. I jumped up. We went together along the gallery, she stopped outside the door. "Aren't you going to put on your things?"

I realised that I must have passed the door of my bedroom, and decided that it was really time for me to learn my way about the house. In my room I found a tweed coat, a hat, scarf, etc., all laid out waiting for me, and a shooting stick as well. I dressed, surveyed my reflection in the glass, and thought that I appeared very smart. I now knew that this was a shooting party. I had seen pictures of such gatherings in newspapers; now I was going to join one. It was most exciting.

When I was ready I ran down to the hall, where I found Mrs Forrester and Phyllis and two other ladies, one fat and old, one short, slim and of vague age. I decided that the fat one was probably 'Old Cissie,' or 'Mrs Darnelton.'

'Old Cissie's' face seemed vaguely familiar. They both said, "Good morning," and then one added something about how energetic it was of us to walk. She had a slight accent of some kind. I felt that she was probably a foreigner.

"We ought to be off," said Mrs Forrester, looking at her watch.

"Au revoir soon," said the foreign lady.

"If Leonora gets up in time," said 'Old Cissie' in a deep voice.

"Oh, start without her if she doesn't," laughed Phyllis.

We three pedestrians started off. It was a cold, bright day, and we went fast. I found it easier to walk quickly in this incarnation than I usually do, and enjoyed it. I allowed the other two to do most of the talking and listened carefully for any remarks that would help me to play my part.

We went down the drive and over a road and through some fields. I thought them very muddy, but the others did not appear to mind. Somebody, I reflected, would have a good stiff job cleaning my shoes that night.

"I wonder if old Potty has killed anyone this morning?" asked Phyllis as we went through a gate.

"Good heavens, is there any danger of that?" said I, startled. Both the others laughed.

Mrs Forrester remarked: "He gets a bit absent sometimes when he's thinking out his next speech."

"Potty incubates his speeches for about three months before he inflicts them on a long suffering public," started Phyllis, and added, "which seems waste of labour because nobody ever pays any attention to what he says."

"Oh, I don't know." This came from Mrs Forrester.

"I believe that large sections of the community take him quite seriously. After all he's honest, and says truthfully what he means."

"I wish he'd declare truthfully at bridge," said Phyllis. "Last night he put me up to five diamonds without a quick trick in his hand."

"How many diamonds had he?" I queried.

"Hello, Eliza, since when did you take an interest in bridge?" asked Phyllis.

"Oh, one hears it discussed," said I, making a mental note that Lady Elizabeth did not play.

"By Mrs Darnelton, for instance," said Phyllis, smiling.

"Mrs Darnelton plays very well," said Mrs Forrester.

"So does he, most Americans do," rejoined Phyllis.

"Americans either play games very well or not at all, there's no bumble-puppy about them," remarked Mrs Forrester.

So Mrs Darnelton was an American. I should never have guessed it from the way in which she spoke. I had heard Americans in plays, or on the talkies, and even real ones in shops, but none of them talked like she did. I also noted that there was a male Darnelton. I wondered how I was to know which man was which when we arrived at wherever we were going, and what I should call them all. I only felt sure of recognising 'Gerald.' We went through another gate and masses of more mud, and came to a farm-house. It seemed to be surrounded by armies of rough looking men.

"There are the beaters. We shall soon have lunch at any rate," said Phyllis.

As we came nearer some of the better dressed men of the crowd moved in our direction.

"Good-mornings," were said to us on all sides. I smiled vaguely at a good many gentlemen, and had my hand shaken by one or two. Then 'Gerald' appeared from somewhere; as I had expected to do, I recognised him from his likeness to the photograph I had seen. He was tall and thin and a little older than in his picture. His clothes did not look new, but they seemed to fit him very well. He was frowning.

"Aren't you rather late, Elizabeth?" He had a deep voice; I thought how nice it would sound if he were not cross.

"Am I?" I queried, feebly.

"The car isn't here yet," said Phyllis, with a funny little smile.

"We always think the ladies are late because their presence is so anxiously awaited," said a broad, rather red-faced man. His accent was just a little American, so I guessed that he must be Mr Darnelton. An oldish gentleman now came up and began to talk to me.

"A very good morning's shooting, Lady Elizabeth, pheasants flew well."

"I'm so glad," said I, at random.

He went on talking about 'coverts' and 'stands' and what happened last year. I wondered if this could be old Potty. I thought it very likely.

"Here comes the car," said someone.

Bumping up the lane, through the mud and over the rough bits of field came the very same car that I had seen in September outside our house. When it stopped, the two ladies I had met in the hall got out of it, and one other. "Now for Leonora," thought I, and looked particularly at her. I knew her at once when she came nearer, I had so often seen her portrait in the newspapers. Lady Giles Gilray. She was very slim and slinky, with hair like shiny copper and extraordinary golden brown eyes; her face was very white, her lips scarlet. She was smoking a cigarette in a long holder.

"I'm afraid we're late," said 'Old Cissie.'

"But Leonora kept us waiting."

Gerald answered, "I'm sure she did, Lady Pottlesham. Leonora never can manage to get up in the morning." His voice, however, did not sound at all angry, and he smiled at Lady Giles.

I turned and gazed at 'Old Cissie.' Lady Pottlesham! No wonder her face had seemed familiar. I had seen her open a Bazaar at West Wampton, and seen pictures of her on platforms at public meetings, accompanying the Earl of Pottlesham.

Tom loved the Earl's speeches, and used often to say that he ought to be Prime Minister. Could the famous Earl of Pottlesham be 'Old Potty?'

"Are we never going to have lunch, Elizabeth?" Gerald's voice sounded cross again.

"Oh—when you like." I looked round wildly, wondering where on earth this enormous party was going to feed.

"Come along." Mrs Forrester took my arm and there was a move towards the farm-house. I realised then that the rough looking men did not belong to the party. I supposed they must be something to do with the shoot. We passed rows and rows of dead pheasants laid out on the grass; there were hares and rabbits too, but fewer.

We arrived in the parlour of the farm-house and sat round the table.

Everybody just plumped down anyhow, not a lady next to a gentleman as might have been expected. There was an empty chair next to mine.

"I suppose I must leave the place of honour for Lord Pottlesham?" said a fair, rather good-looking man with crinkly hair, to me.

Lord Pottlesham hurried into the room, looking a little less impressive than he does in the papers, because of his wearing a tweed suit. "Sorry, Elizabeth, I was just giving Barker some instructions."

He sat down beside me, rubbing his hands.

"Terribly hungry weather, isn't it? I'm going to eat an enormous lunch."

I was so overawed that I could not answer him.

VI

It did feel strange to be suddenly sitting like that next to a celebrity. I did not know what to call him. He called me Elizabeth, but then he was much older than I was. How did one address Earls?

On my other side sat a much younger man with a pale face and rather curious grey eyes, who had said, "How do you do?" to me when I first arrived. He talked to me about quite ordinary things, but I was too busy thinking of Lord Pottlesham to pay much attention to him, and soon he got caught up in a conversation with the old gentleman next to him, the one who had talked to me about coverts, whom some of them called 'Horton' and some 'Sir Edward.'

As they were busy talking and as Lord Pottlesham was very much occupied with eating, I was able to have a good look round. I thought it seemed rather a common sort of lunch to give such grand people. Irish stew, beefsteak and kidney pudding, potatoes in jackets, though all very good of their kind, I must say.

The servants handing the dishes wore no livery, and there was no champagne. I had thought that rich people always drank champagne at parties, but most of them seemed to be drinking beer or whiskey and soda, or even water, though there was wine.

Lady Giles drank beer. She was sitting next to Gerald, who had a man with whiskers on his other side. I could see that she was making him laugh a good deal.

Everybody talked and seemed cheerful. I noticed Phyllis by the side of a young man with brown hair and eyes, and rather a long nose. I felt sure it must be 'Toby.' He looked at her as though he liked her very much, and I thought that she would be quite right if she married him.

When the plum-pudding came, Lord Pottlesham seemed to be a little less hungry, and turned to me. He asked me some questions about the garden. I felt that it was a pity to waste him on gardening, and asked him straight out about something in one of his speeches that had interested Tom. He looked pleased, and a little surprised.

So you read that speech, Elizabeth?"

"No, I heard it on the wireless."

He looked astonished.

"I thought you disliked 'quacking' on the wireless?"

"I wanted to hear you," I said. It was Tom who had, really, but I could hardly explain that. He seemed delighted, and launched out into a positive flood of talk, telling me all kinds of things that I knew would thrill Tom. I listened with all my ears, trying to remember as much as I could of his statements, and never noticed that the other people had been getting more and more silent, until Gerald's voice came coldly across the table.

"Sorry to interrupt you, Elizabeth, but time's getting on."

I felt vexed. Gerald was an attractive man, but I did not every day have the chance of talking to a real live Cabinet Minister about important things, so I snapped:

"I was having a very interesting conversation with Lord Pottlesham."

Gerald's eyebrows went up. Lord Pottlesham beamed.

"Gerald's right, my dear Elizabeth. Days are short this time of year, we can resume our chat later."

"Oh, I do hope so," I exclaimed sincerely.

Everybody got up and we all went out. Men carrying guns were waiting, but the rough crowd had disappeared. Phyllis came laughing up to me.

"You are full of surprises to-day, Eliza. Old Potty hasn't been listened to like that for years."

"But surely he's a very great man?" I quoted Tom.

She giggled as though I had made a joke.

We moved on in a little army: men and dogs and guns. I saw Brandon ahead following Gerald, who walked beside Leonora.

Toby and Phyllis approached me, she slipped her hand through his arm. "Toby, my sweet." (So I had guessed right.) "Elizabeth gave me advice about us this morning."

He seemed a little nervous. "Oh—of course. Elizabeth could not be expected to see—"

"Wrong for once, my angel, Elizabeth favoured love in a cottage."

His face lit up. "Oh—do you really think—"

I felt confused at the idea of discussing such intimate matters with a stranger, but Phyllis broke in before I could speak:

"I haven't said I agree with her yet, Toby."

"This way, sir." A man, whom I took to be a gamekeeper, directed Toby towards a certain spot in the field. He and Phyllis left me.

We were all near a wood now, and people were dividing into little groups of two's and three's at some distance from each other. The fair, crinkly haired man said to me, "Are you coming to talk to me, Lady Elizabeth?" He looked better tempered than Gerald, I thought, and I liked his blue eyes. I wondered though if I ought not to join Gerald who was talking to Leonora a little way off. I hesitated.

"Be kind to a stranger and sit on this." He opened his shooting stick.

"Oh—I've got a shooting stick too."

"Never mind, try mine, I think you'll find it comfortable."

I thanked him and sat down, feeling rather like a bird on a perch. He told me how pleased he was to have been free to-day and able to accept 'Forrester's' invitation to shoot. I supposed he must be the 'Champion Man,' that Mrs Forrester had talked of earlier in the day. "A bit of a bounder," she had called him. I wondered why; he seemed very easy to get on with, very friendly, and made me giggle several times.

"Have a cigarette?" He offered me his case.

"No, thanks."

"Off your smoke?"

"I suppose so."

It was strange, but now he mentioned it, I was conscious of a strange sort of hankering for a cigarette; it was as though my body wanted one while my mind did not. I decided not to risk it, I felt a little full of lunch, which is unusual with me.

I wondered at last when the people were going after the birds, and why they waited such a long time. Then suddenly there came a whistle from the wood, Mr Champion stopped talking, seemed to stiffen all over, made a little click with his gun and stood in front of me.

Then came noises and whirring sounds. A bird flew out of the wood, somebody shouted, "Over," there was an awful bang and the bird fell stone dead.

"Oh, the poor thing," I cried.

Then everything started happening. The whole sky seemed to be full of flying little bodies; shouts and cries issued from the wood, guns banged all round, and birds fell with flops all over the place. I was so frightened that I shook in every limb. "Oh, don't—don't," I squeaked as the poor creatures fell. One of them near to me fluttered and fluttered on the ground, a dog ran after it, caught it, and brought it, with its wings still flapping, to a man who wrung its neck.

I screamed. I could not help it, hid my eyes and burst into tears. The next thing I heard was the fair man's distressed voice. "Lady Elizabeth—for Heaven's sake, what's the matter?"

"Oh, go away, go away," I sobbed.

"But—Lady Elizabeth—"

"Go away, don't talk to me."

I suppose he went, and before long Gerald was beside me. "What on earth's the matter, Elizabeth?" His voice sounded half angry and half anxious. He put his hand on my arm. I shook it off, sobbing too hard to speak.

"For God's sake pull yourself together; tell me what's up. Are you ill?"

"The poor things—the poor things, it's so cruel," I gasped.

"What on earth are you talking about? Do try and control yourself."

Mrs Forrester, who always seemed to turn up when I was in difficulties, now came on the scene.

"My dear, it's all right." Her arm went round me; it felt very gentle. I clung to her.

"Take me away."

"Of course, dear."

"What's wrong, can I be of any use?" Leonora had strolled up.

"Nothing's wrong," said Mrs Forrester, sharply.

"Elizabeth's got a bad headache, the guns were too much for her."

I mopped my eyes and sniffed. I was better, though still trembling. Gerald, standing in front of us, was frowning. Leonora at his side looked surprised and interested. Nobody else had come near.

I longed for home and Tom with all my heart. Oh, to get away from those poor dead birds and those strange people.

"Darling, you've been overdoing it," said Lady Giles. She had a very deep voice with a musical rise in it. "Why don't you go back and have some sal volatile or something?"

"She's all right now," said Mrs Forrester quickly. "Aren't you dear?"

"I'd like to go home," I said, in a low voice.

"Can't I come with you? I'm terribly good about nerves," said Leonora.

"Elizabeth's not given to nerves," said Gerald.

"Everyone has nerves, darling," she said. "I know a perfectly wonderful man—"

"I'm not ill, I just want to go home," I insisted.

"I'll come with you."

"Will you, now," said Gerald's mother. "Come, Gerald, you go and look after the others."

He hesitated. "Are you all right, Elizabeth?"

"I shall be," I answered.

"Hurry up, Gerald." Mrs Forrester sounded impatient. "We shall have everybody wondering what's up, and it's really nothing. Come, Elizabeth."

She drew me away from the scene of carnage, paying no attention to Leonora's advice of bed and doctor for me, which floated musically after us.

My only desire was for escape. I thought of my home with all my might, but no dizzy feeling came. We walked faster and faster till we came to the farmhouse. I hiccuped at intervals, as I always do after crying. When we reached the farmhouse the big car was standing waiting, and the fair-haired shooter was there too.

"I nipped on and fetched the car. I thought you might want it."

"Thank you, Captain Champion," said Mrs Forrester drily.

Captain Champion looked sympathetically at me. "Is there anything I can do, Lady Elizabeth?"

"No, thank you."

"I'm awfully sorry you are seedy, half the pleasure of the day will be gone now you're not there!"

"Thanks for finding us the car."

"You'd better hurry back to the others now, or they'll think you're lost," said the old lady crisply.

Soon we were in the car and bumping away.

"I thought Champion wanted to come too," said Mrs Forrester with a little laugh.

"He was kind," I murmured.

"Oh, he means well, I've no doubt. Certainly he's an excellent shot."

I shuddered a little.

"Cold, dear?"

"Oh no, thanks."

We bumped on to the main road, and purred away towards Heringdon.

VII

The realisation came to me that I was now actually inside the very car that I had longed to glide away in, on that evening which now seemed so far away. My wish had come true. I was on my way to a comfortable house and was not enjoying myself at all.

It is true that the first vividness of the shock and horror caused by the shoot was fading. As I thought things over it did not seem so terrible. After all, the birds had died quickly, even the fluttering one had not been left long in pain.

All those people who seemed quite pleasant and ordinary had taken the massacre as a matter of course. Only I had never seen things killed, except on the films, when naturally one knows that it does not hurt. I had never enjoyed animal films much if wild beasts were shot, even though they were savage leopards and tigers and lions. Of course I had known that such things took place; that the meat people eat gets knocked on the head, and chickens have their necks wrung, but I had never visualised what slaughter was actually like. I simply had never thought about it.

When we arrived at Heringdon Mrs Forrester took me up to my room and bustled me into bed. When she rang the bell a smart-looking woman appeared who turned out to be a lady's maid who was called Foley.

Foley got hot water bottles, and found me a lovely nightdress which seemed to be made of lace and gossamer. I admired it very much, but it was so thin that it made me feel quite shy, and I was glad when she gave me a lacy kind of little coat to put over it. There was a beautiful fire burning, and the bed was wonderfully soft and comfortable, with what felt like crowds of pillows.

I was glad of the hot water bottle, as the sheets felt so very cool and smooth. They were made of extremely fine linen, and had a monogram "E.F." on the part that turns down. There were monograms on the pillows too. The bed itself was a four-poster, the "roof" seemed miles above my head when I looked up, and I thought how lucky it was that the room was so high. A silver lamp hung from the top of the bed. The day bed-cover had been taken away and in its place was a lovely bedspread of feathers, ever so light and warm.

Mrs Forrester seemed pleased when I had settled down, and said: "That's better, isn't it? Now what about sending for Doctor Sellyn?"

"Good Heavens, no," I exclaimed in terror.

"Darling, you must be very seedy, or you, of all people, would never have broken down like that in public."

"I'm not seedy. I only hated seeing the poor birds killed."

"My dear, don't talk nonsense, tell me is there anything—*really* the matter, anything that Sellyn ought to know about?" Her eyes were fixed on mine. I felt inclined to laugh. What would she say if I told her, "All that's *really* the matter with me is that I'm not *me* at all."

However, I restrained myself, and assured her that I would soon be all right, and absolutely refused to see the doctor.

She suggested several things that I might take, and I told her that all I really wanted was a cup of good hot tea with plenty of milk and sugar. At that, she seemed to think that I was making fun of her, which, of course, I was not, because I can always do with a cup of tea. Finally I convinced her that all I needed was rest, and she went away.

Then with all my might and main I tried to wish myself back in my own skin, and my own surroundings. I willed so hard for my trance to stop that I almost made myself sick; without result.

My heart thumped with fear. Was I doomed to be Lady Elizabeth for

- 48 -

ever? A cold sweat broke out all over me. Impossible, the previous attacks had ended, this one must do so too, yet it had lasted a horribly long time.

What was happening at home? Were the children all right? I felt helpless. Tears of exasperation and fear burned my eyelids. I began to think over various ways of escape from Heringdon if the trance went on. Foley would find me clothes, but how was I to get hold of money; find my way to the station; would anybody at home know me if I returned there? I do not know how long I lay worrying and crying.

After a while there was a knock on the door. I gulped and wiped my eyes; another knock, the door opened softly and Gerald's voice asked in a low tone, "Are you asleep?"

"No."

He came up to the bed. I felt myself blushing. Of course it was quite proper for him to be there, because he thought I was his wife, but I could not help knowing that I was Polly Wilkinson, and that he was a strange man. I felt uncomfortable, and a little angry with him as well. Tom would never have gone on shooting for the rest of the afternoon, knowing me to be upset, and perhaps ill.

He enquired how I was. I told him nothing was the matter.

"Something must be. I've never known you make a scene before."

"Did I make a scene?"

"What else would you call it?"

Suddenly I was annoyed. "Have you never seen a woman cry in your life?"

"Not you."

"Perhaps you are unobservant."

"Do you weep in secret, my dear?" His voice sounded sarcastic. He prepared to sit on the edge of the bed.

"Don't do that," I snapped out, thinking of what Tom would feel, if he knew.

His eyebrows went up; they were a nice shape, brown and thick without being heavy, one arched a little higher than the other when they rose.

"Your nerves are certainly in a bad state. I should advise you to have a good rest."

"Perhaps I could if I was left alone."

He seemed taken aback. "I have certainly no desire to disturb you. I trust you will be better by dinner time." He spoke very politely, but I could see that he was offended. I did not mind if he were. He went.

Just as he shut the door the blessed giddiness came. When things were steady again, I felt Tom's arms round me, and saw his anxious face close to mine.

"Polly—Polly, my darling, my sweetie, what is the matter?"

I felt as if people had been asking me that all day.

"Oh Tom, Tom, thank God." I clung to him, and burst into tears.

He hugged and kissed me while I hung on to him as if I would never let him go. There is always something comforting about Tom if one is upset. He was sweet, and soon I calmed down; but it was a little difficult to explain my agitation to him. I told him that I had been worrying, which was certainly true.

"You must have been, sweetheart, but why did that make you look at me as if I were a stranger when I came in?"

"Did I, Tom?"

"Yes, and when I kissed you, you fainted."

"It wasn't really fainting, Tom, only a little giddiness."

"What has been frightening my kiddy girl?"

"Well—you were away so long, and—"

"But you knew when I was coming back, honeysuckle."

I nearly replied that I had no idea where I was! I looked round our sitting room, and felt as if the furniture and ornaments were all gazing at me with friendly expressions.

"Oh, it's lovely to be back—I mean—to have you back Tommy—boy."

He hugged me again and began to tell me about his trip; he thought he had done a good stroke of work. Bendale would be pleased. A thought flashed across my mind—the children. I interrupted Tom's discourse.

"Just one moment, Tommy, I must run and have a look at the kiddies to see if they are all right."

"Why shouldn't they be?"

"Just a moment, precious, I'll be back directly."

He caught my arm. "You've had the brats with you the whole blessed time I've been away. Surely they can be left alone for a minute. Then I'll come and see them with you."

"But Tommy—"

"Oh well, if you don't want to hear my news—" He loosed my arm, and I hurried from the room, reflecting that I had offended two husbands in one day, a record for any woman.

The children were in the next room playing a complicated game with bricks and toy soldiers. They clamoured for a boat which they seemed to think I had gone to fetch and, though pleased to hear of Daddy's return, showed no inclination to come and see him.

Betty suggested that he should come and play too. "It is such a lovely game, and I've built the castle like you said."

"Drinlaw Castle, where the chief lives," added Bobby.

"Daddy will make you a boat, and we'll finish the game another time, pets."

I managed to get them into the other room, but I had some difficulty in turning their minds from the game, which seemed to have caught their imaginations thoroughly.

Luckily bed time came at last. Tom was very stiff in his manner at supper time, and grumbled about kids being brought up to think themselves the centre of the universe, which was unfair, because, if either of us spoils them, it is he; I have them on my hands all day.

It was some time before he unbent and told me all about his success in

Manchester. After supper he was put out of humour, because he could not find his new tin of cigarettes, and when he did, he discovered that it had been opened, and some cigarettes taken.

He surmised that the culprit must be Gladys, as he knew I did not smoke, unless I had had friends in.

I denied visitors and assured him that Gladys did not smoke.

"Perhaps her young man does," he snorted.

My heart was beating hard; the whole truth had begun to dawn on me.

When I went to help Gladys wash up, I sounded her about the cigarettes carefully, because she is touchy, and satisfied myself that she had not taken any. She seemed subdued, and more civil than usual. She remembered seeing the unopened tin before Tom left and could not understand its present condition.

I knew Lady Elizabeth smoked; so much that people remarked on it when she did not. There was a real Lady Elizabeth, and she and I changed places!

While I had been having adventures at Heringdon she had been in my home. How had that never occurred to me before? Of course, it was she who had played with the children, and snubbed Ethel, and—been kissed by Tom on his return from Manchester. Fury swept over me. How dared she come into my home, tell my children stories, put them to bed, kiss Tom, and smoke his cigarettes! It was all very well my going to Heringdon, but to have someone here, at home, masquerading about in my skin, among my family, was a different matter. How had it happened? I tried to remember the beginning of it all. The migrations had always occurred when I had been thinking of Heringdon, and I had generally been thinking of home when I returned,—but not always; to-day, for instance, I had longed to escape, ages before I had been able to do so. Had she strange powers over me? Did she regulate those psychic journeys? Why in the world did she choose me to experiment on? Should I write and ask her? I quailed at the thought of doing so. If I went to a perfect stranger with a story like mine I should not be believed. I could not prove any statement that I could make.

She would only have to deny everything. There was no one in the world who could help me. I resolved to put every thought concerning her, and her house, away from me. If it came to a battle of wills, I was determined to win.

VIII

Jorkins came to supper on that evening, and he and Tom talked politics, as they generally did; but on this occasion I was able to join in their conversation. I let off some of the things that 'Old Potty' had told me, and surprised them both.

"How do you know that, Mrs Tom?" asked Jorkins, after one of my pronouncements.

"Oh, Lord Pottlesham told me so himself," I answered, adding, "you see, I sat next to him at lunch to-day."

They both laughed at that, and Jorkins chaffed me about my grand acquaintances, and asked when the Earl was next expected to drop in.

Talking of Lord Pottlesham reminded me of Lady Elizabeth's existence, and I had a momentary fear of being switched back into it, but all was well. I kept Tom awake in bed that night for a long time, and made him tell me all sorts of things, concentrating my mind hard on his conversation. What would happen if Elizabeth experimented in the middle of the night?

She seemed, however, to have decided to leave me in peace, and my days passed in their normal busily uneventful way, with Christmas looming before me. Preparations for that took up most of my attention, so that I had little time in which to remember Heringdon.

On one evening, though, it was brought back to my mind in spite of myself. I had been shopping in Town, and Tom and I, and our friends, the Burgesses, ended the day at the theatre. I saw Gerald and Leonora in a box. She had on a lovely evening coat with white fur. They were quite alone, just the two of them.

After my first fear that I should be translated into Elizabeth, and miss the play, I watched them with interest. We had a very good view of them from the dress circle, where our seats were.

"That's a good looking woman," said Tom, "though a bit on the thin side, perhaps."

"It's Lady Giles Gilray, wife of the celebrated polo player," said Wally Burgess.

"Wally cuts her photos out of the paper," said Wally's mother. "He envies the celebrated polo player, don't you, Wal?"

"I suppose that's the husband with her," said Tom.

"Oh, no, it isn't." The words slipped out before I could stop them. "It's Major Gerald Forrester."

"How do you know that, Polly?" asked Annie Burgess.

"Oh—just by the papers—" I was a little confused.

"I hope you don't cut his pictures out, he's a handsome man. What do you say, Tom?" Annie went on teasingly.

"Looks as hard as nails to me," grunted Tom.

Just then the curtain went up again.

I wondered if Elizabeth knew what Gerald was doing, and if Leonora's husband minded her going out with a married man like that!

It was no good. I was too much interested in all their lives to keep my mind off them; and next day and all the days after that, I looked in the papers to see if I could find any details about them, or any of the other people I had met. I was particularly anxious to see something about Phyllis and Toby, but, knowing neither of their surnames, tracing them through the columns of the press was difficult.

I read a speech of Lord Pottlesham's and saw that Mr and Mrs Angell B. Darnelton were entertaining a party for Christmas at Thinnesley Hall, which they had rented from the Marquis of Avon; and that Sir Edward Horton's 'Rainbow' had won something or other steeplechase.

In spite of the terror that my last visit there had caused me, I began to wish for some further explorations into the Heringdon world. The fear of being whisked away from my surroundings alternated with a feeling that life would be very flat if I was not.

Christmas Day arrived. Tom's brother and sister-in-law came to dinner with their kids, also Aunt Abigail and Cousin Fanny and Jack Sparlow from the office. Ethel and Sydney had arranged to come in the evening, as they were obliged to dine with Syd's father and mother.

Dinner went off very well. Tom was in great spirits because he had got his rise, a big one, £55. He had bought a goose, and of course we had plum pudding; George and Mabel had brought two bottles of champagne, so we had those as well as the port wine. We laughed a lot and pulled the crackers with the kids, and Jack Sparlow told some killingly funny stories, and imitated Mr Bendale to the life.

Only Aunt Abigail said that goose always gave her indigestion, and Cousin Fanny was offended when she had her plum pudding on a cold plate by mistake.

After dinner Mr Sparlow and George and Tom took the kiddies for a walk, while Mabel and I helped Gladys to clear up, and put the things ready for tea. Aunt Abigail slept and Fanny went to put the finishing touches to the Christmas tree, which was behind a screen in the sitting room. When Mabel and I had finished, and had got the dining room ready, and Gladys had gone off, as she was spending the evening with her people, we went upstairs to get tidy before the gentlemen came back.

While I was putting my hair tidy and taking the shine off my nose with some powder, my thoughts went to Elizabeth. How was she spending her Christmas Day?—Whisk—In a moment I turned giddy—.

Even through the topsy-turvy feeling, I could hear myself saying,

"Damn." It was too bad, just on Christmas Day, when the children were on their way home to the tree—how dared she—?

I "came to" in a strange room. It did not look like one of those which I already knew. I was sitting on a very large and deep sofa; a man with thick black hair, except for a grey lock on the forehead, was beside me and a young, rather pale, man was sitting on a cushion on the floor, facing me. The last mentioned person was talking in a high voice, about *crescendo* and *pizzicato*, and things like that, which sounded gibberish to me. On the other side of the room were four people playing bridge and I recognised one of them as Mr Darnelton. As I registered all this on my consciousness, the rubber ended. Somebody proposed starting another one, but an oldish lady said, "No," she really could not play any more and got up.

"Oh, Bellows, we must have another one," cried a third woman, "where's Emmeline?"

"Playing in the blue room, I think," said Darnelton. "But I'll go and see who I can find."

"Pity you don't play, Elizabeth," said the third woman.

Did I not? The members of our Bridge Club could tell a different story. Tom and I are very nearly their star players, and Tom solves problems in the papers. Elizabeth did not play. Well, this time she should. I got up from the sofa, saying, "I'll play with pleasure."

They all laughed.

"Like the Irishman who said that he did not know if he could play the fiddle, till he tried," said a gentleman with grey hair and eye-glasses, who was sitting at the table.

"But I mean it," I insisted. I was boiling with anger inside. I did not care what difficulties were created for Elizabeth by my conduct.

"Since when have you taken to cards?" asked the man with the white lock. "I thought you loathed them."

"One may change one's mind," I pronounced.

"The privilege of your sex," said Darnelton, "but seriously—"

"Seriously, I mean it, I'm ready to play here and now." Somehow I convinced them that I was sincere. Darnelton seemed amused, and anxious to try. The thin lady looked doubtful, and the gentleman in glasses displeased. We cut and I had him for my partner.

"What are we playing for?" asked the thin lady.

"Don't let's make it high," growled my partner.

"What were you playing before?" I asked.

"Twopence."

I was surprised. We sometimes go as far as threepence a hundred at home. Certainly these people did not gamble. I signified that the amount would suit me. We began.

There are days, when, while playing bridge, one seems to keep on making mistakes, but there are others when everything one does goes right. This was such an occasion for me.

I wish Tom could have seen me. I took risks and they came off, made bold calls and the results were positively brilliant, every finesse was right, and good cards were my portion as well. I impressed the bridge party thoroughly.

"This *is* staggering," said the thin woman, whom the others called Dora, at the end of a rubber, which I had won for our side with a grand slam, called, doubled, and redoubled, vulnerable.

"Why have you hidden this talent from us all this time?" enquired Darnelton.

"Have you been studying long?" asked the man with the eye-glasses, whom Darnelton called Massey, and Dora addressed as Walter. I wondered if he could be the Colonel Walter Massey who wrote articles on bridge. Later I discovered that he was.

"That's my little secret," I said archly.

Mr Darnelton, or Bellows, as Dora called him, was busy adding up the score. "You win twenty pounds, Elizabeth."

"Twenty p…" I gasped. So these people had been playing twopence a point. Supposing I had lost. Then I remembered that the debt would have been Elizabeth's, and wished I had.

We stopped playing then. Mr Darnelton wrote down the score in a big book. Nobody produced any money.

"What about a cocktail?" he enquired.

Servants had brought in tea, and lots of bottles on trays. Mr Darnelton began to shake cocktails, and ask people what they wanted. I gathered that this was not Heringdon, and guessed that it was Thinnesley Hall, and the Darnelton's Christmas party.

More people came into the room, amongst them Mrs Darnelton, Gerald and Leonora. The universal surprise among the newcomers when they were told that I had been playing bridge was enormous. Gerald refused to believe it.

"You're pulling my leg. Elizabeth's never played in her life, she wouldn't know a heart from a spade."

"All I can tell you is, that she played like a master," said Massey. "Did you really know nothing about it?"

"Gerald doesn't know everything about me," I said, looking up at Elizabeth's husband through my lashes, as Vera Ambrose does in *Money for Jam*.

He stared.

"Have a cocktail, Elizabeth—this is the one you liked yesterday." Darnelton was handing me a glass. I refused it, rejecting a momentary temptation to make Lady Elizabeth tipsy and horrify her friends. I feared that I might give myself away too much, having a weak head for wine. I had drunk half a glass of champagne at my own Christmas dinner, and did not know how much that would affect her body.

"No, thank you, I'll have a good strong cup of tea, if I may."

I went to the table where Mrs Darnelton, or Emmeline, as most of them called her, was pouring out. The tea was even better than the Heringdon one, there were lovely things to eat; it gave me a heartache to see it. My mind flew to the children at home. They would have had their presents off the tree by now, perhaps she, Elizabeth, had given them to them. A wave of anger rose in me. I longed to teach her a lesson. My appetite was gone and I wanted to cry. The man with the white lock of hair came up to me. He seemed displeased about something.

"Here's your tea, Mr Buschner, with lemon, as you like it." Mrs Darnelton handed him a cup, which he took, bowing a little.

Buschner, where had I heard that name? Memory brought it back to me; big letters outside the Albert Hall, Ethel's Sydney going to concerts, telling us about him. Syd had even tried to get Tom and me to go and hear him once; but we thought an entertainment consisting of only one man playing the piano for a whole afternoon would be very dry.

At any rate he was a celebrity; my interest in my surroundings began to revive. If only it had not been Christmas Day, I should have enjoyed myself.

Leonora glided up from somewhere. "What have you been doing all the afternoon, Buschner?" she asked.

"Lady Elizabeth, Hardleigh and I were talking until she deserted us for the card table." He spoke with a foreign accent.

"You must have bored her to make her do anything so desperate," drawled Lady Giles.

"That is a little what I felt," Mr Buschner frowned.

"To tell the truth," I announced cheerfully, "I really don't remember what Mr Buschner and Mr—er—Hardleigh were talking about."

"Oh, surely you don't mean that," said Emmeline, while Leonora's laugh gurgled out. It is a lovely laugh, as musical as her voice.

"Really, Buschner, you will have to take lessons in the art of conversation," she said.

"Perhaps it was my fault," chipped in Mr Hardleigh in his high voice. "I talked more than my share."

"Don't let them tease you, Mr Buschner. Leonora, you are really too bad, and I'm surprised by Elizabeth." Emmeline smiled soothingly at everybody.

Mr Buschner unscowled, and shrugged his shoulders. "Perhaps Christmas is apt to be trying," he said.

"Are you going to make it more tolerable for us by playing?" asked Leonora.

He looked coldly at her. "I do not know if I am in the mood."

"That's your fault, darling," said Lady Giles to me. "You've upset him, and I thought that you certainly could persuade him to enchant us."

There was something in her tone I did not like, so I said bluntly: "Why me? I'm sure that you can do more with gentlemen than I can. Ask Gerald."

There was a dead silence.

IX

Everybody seemed uncomfortable. I did not mind. I had been torn from my home on Christmas Day, and did not care what mischief I made. I took a sandwich and bit into it. Gerald laughed, though I could see he was angry.

"Elizabeth's right, Leonora could wile a bird off a bush. Have a cigarette?" He offered her his case.

She said "Ta," and took one.

"I will play to you now," announced Mr Buschner, seeming suddenly much more cheerful.

"Ah, how divine of you," Mrs Darnelton cried in a delighted voice, springing to her feet. Exclamations of pleasure came from all round.

"Come along." Emmeline led the way to a big room; I was surprised at the small amount of furniture there was in it. Mr Buschner sat down before a piano, which Mr Hardleigh had opened for him, shook the white lock off his forehead, and began to play.

He played something that sounded very difficult, with crashing noises and lots of runs; I wished Sydney had been there, he would probably have liked it.

When Mr Buschner stopped, murmurs of "Marvellous. Wonderful. How divine," and things like that came from all over the room.

"Miraculous," sighed Mr Hardleigh, turning up his pale blue eyes. "No one plays Ostrosch as you do, Maestro."

Buschner smiled at me. "What shall I play now? Choose, Elizabeth."

"Something with a tune in it for Heaven's sake, I can't make head or tail of those noises," I cried.

The pianist got off the music stool with such violence that it flew across the bare boards of the room. He strode over to me with his black eyes sparkling, and exclaimed furiously, "What have I done to you that you insult me?"

"Oh, please, Mr Buschner," Emmeline hurried up to him. "I'm sure Elizabeth was only chaffing, we were all loving it so."

"I said just what I thought," I declared, opening my eyes very wide, and trying to look innocent like Marina Moyhala, in *Cherry Lips*. "I'm sorry if I offended you."

He glared at me.

"Oh! do play again, Maestro," said Mr Hardleigh—his voice was a positive wail.

"Chuck playing the ass, Elizabeth," said Gerald crossly. "A joke's all very well, but—"

"Don't talk to me like that, I won't have it. Can't I say what I think? It's a free country," I said.

"Please go back to the piano, we are dying to hear you," pleaded Emmeline.

I felt sorry for her, but I was too cross to be amiable to any of these strangers among whom I was an unwilling prisoner. Elizabeth should get the blame for my ill manners. She would have to put things straight all round. Viciously I hoped she would find it difficult.

From nearly everybody came pleas for Mr Buschner to continue playing.

"What would you like? A Christmas carol?" he demanded fiercely.

"That would be lovely," I said, trying to look under my lashes again. It was fun having long lashes to look through.

He said something under his breath that I felt sure was not polite, went to the piano and crashed out *Good King Wenceslas*. He played it in a very funny way, putting in all sorts of runs and high notes, and the audience began to laugh. "Well?" he asked when he had finished.

"It's a pity to spoil a good tune like that," I said gravely, and they laughed again.

"Perhaps you prefer this?" He played *My Pretty Daisy* from *That's the Girl*, not looking at the piano at all, thumping the notes hard and scowling.

My Pretty Daisy is one of Tom's favourite tunes; he has it on a gramophone record, and at the thought that at that very moment he might be playing it I could bear no more. I jumped up and stamped my foot, crying, "Stop it! Stop it!"

He wheeled round on the music stool. "Isn't that the music you prefer to Ostrosch?"

"Much; but not like that, you ruin it."

He leaped up again, his face quite white. "I think for the present I had better play no more."

Protests came from everywhere, but Mr Buschner paid no attention to them. He passed his hand over his forehead. "I am no more in the mood. I am tired. I think I will rest before dinner." He made a stiff sort of bow to Mrs Darnelton and left the room.

"Oh dear," said poor Emmeline. "How could you, Elizabeth?"

"Genius baiting is a new departure of yours, like bridge, isn't it, darling?" asked Leonora. "But why do you spring them both on us in one afternoon? We're really not strong enough to stand it." She laughed softly.

"I was longing to hear more Ostrosch," moaned Mr Hardleigh.

"Why not take a ticket for his next concert," I snapped.

"I think your sense of humour is a bit out of hand, my dear," said Gerald drily. "I doubt if any of us, especially Emmeline, appreciate it."

"That's enough from you," said I, tartly. "You don't look as though you had a sense of humour at all."

There was a laugh or two at that, and Leonora chuckled. "One for you, Gerald. Do you often tick him off like that, darling?"

Gerald spoke before I could answer. "I don't think this is particularly amusing. What about a game of backgammon before dinner?"

She agreed and they went off together. The others seemed to disperse. Emmeline Darnelton put her hand on my arm.

"Elizabeth, what has Buschner done?" she asked in a low voice.

"Nothing that I know of," I said, with the Marina Moyhala look.

"I rather wish you had not upset him then," she sighed. "He's very difficult to get, and I did so hope he would play."

"Oh, I expect he will," I said cheerfully.

She went on. "I'm glad you think so. Of course, you know him very well. When I told him you were coming, he said that you were one of the few women he knew who really understood music."

"Oh—I don't know about that. I know what I like, of course."

She looked at me in a puzzled sort of way. Bellows came in.

"I hear that the musical party has broken up," he said. "These artists are so temperamental."

"Weren't you there?" I enquired.

He shook his head. "I'm afraid I'm no good at this highbrow music. Emmeline's crazy about it. I thought you were too."

"I wasn't this afternoon."

"Do we play some more bridge?" asked Darnelton.

"It's getting late, Bellows," said his wife. "You know how that rubber before dinner has a way of never ending."

A footman came in and spoke to Mrs Darnelton. "Oh, bother, the Rockleys have chucked us. She's got influenza. That means rearranging all the dinner cards." She bustled from the room.

"I'm sorry," said Darnelton. "I know you'd have liked to see them. They're an acquisition to the neighbourhood, don't you think?"

"Oh, are they—"

He looked questioningly at me. "Well, the first time I met him was at your shoot, when he came over from Merefield." He then looked embarrassed. "Of course, I'd forgotten, you were ill then."

Just then someone came to the door and shouted, "Bellows, come and help," and he was swept away to arbitrate in a bridge dispute.

Left alone, I reflected on my plight. Here I was in a strange house, not knowing the way to my room, with no fore-knowledge of the moment that would bring my escape. I had upset the hostess and one of her principal guests. What should I do now? Perhaps it would be better to find some of the others and wait on events.

I left the music room, and found myself in a passage with doors on each side. I opened one at random and found myself in a small room full of bookcases.

Mr Buschner sprang up from a sofa—he was alone.

"Ah, you guessed I would be here?" he exclaimed.

"No, I didn't, I merely lost my way. I'm sorry if I've disturbed you."

"Tell me what I have done. Why are you angry with me?"

"But I'm not."

"You tell me that you do not like Ostrosch's Rhapsody in B minor, when I play it for you as I have never played it before! You tell me that before a whole roomful of fools. Why?"

"Oh—I don't quite know." My tone was weak. "How have I offended?"

"Well—I don't think you have." He calmed down a little, but he was looking at me very intently. "It is not like you to vent your anger on the wrong person."

"I'm afraid I don't understand."

"Ach, why do you always hide behind a mask, Elizabeth?" His voice shook a little, he spoke very earnestly. "You know, you must always have known, the things I want to say to you. The things I feel, that I tell you when I play."

I was rather shocked and a little bit thrilled too; he was trying to make love to me.

"I don't think you ought to talk to me like that, Mr Buschner." His face grew stern, an angry vein stood out on his forehead.

"Why are you changed, why are you so different? Always you are aloof and remote, yes, but there has been sympathy between us. Why are you trying to hurt me, when you know how much you mean to me?"

"Aren't you forgetting that I'm a married woman?"

"My God—are you going to tell me that it is for the sake of that conceited stick that you are being cruel to me; that you are really angry because he fetches and carries for the imitation vamp? They are toy people, not worth our notice."

He poured all this out in a verbal flood, before I could stop him.

"Really, Mr Buschner, I'm surprised at your talking like this. Major Forrester may have his faults, but he is my husband, and I can't listen to—"

He made a sudden fierce movement which quite startled me. "How dare you laugh at me."

"But I'm not, I'm talking quite seriously. Please do be calm."

He clenched his fists by his sides, and breathed deeply. "Elizabeth, if you were not so beautiful, I would wring your neck."

A gong boomed somewhere at that moment.

"Oh, good gracious, is that supper, I mean dinner?" I cried.

"Dressing gong," he answered briefly. "Such is life, drama, and another meal."

"Oh, do let's go and dress, I'm sure you'll feel ever so much better afterwards—after dinner I mean—gentlemen generally do."

I went to the door; he opened it, bowed me through, then shut it between us rather hard. I found myself faced with the problem of finding my bedroom.

Up a staircase I went, and through what felt like miles of passages. There were little tickets on most of the doors, with names written on them, but never mine.

Finally I met a housemaid. I stopped her. "Oh, excuse me, it's really very silly, but I've lost the way to my room."

Her eyes opened so wide that I thought they would drop out of her face, but, having mastered my name, or rather my temporary one, she led me to the door which bore my label.

I thanked her and went into the indicated room. As I entered it, Gerald got out of an armchair near the fire.

X

"Oh," was all that I could find to say. Gerald was frowning heavily, and his mouth looked very stern. I had a feeling that, if he was really my husband, I should be a tiny bit frightened of him when he looked like that.

"I want to talk to you, Elizabeth," he began.

"Won't we be late for dinner?"

"Never mind that, Dora's sure to be later. Tell me, what the devil are you playing at?"

"I am not playing at anything."

"Then why did you behave in that extraordinary way?"

"What did I do that was unusual?"

"What the hell made you rag Buschner like you did, when Emmeline wanted him to play, and snap my head off as well?"

"Can't I talk to you as I like?"

"Explain the meaning of all this. You'd better tell me, my dear. If you are going to acquire a habit of making scenes in public I shall clear out. That's one thing I won't stand."

"You'd clear out with your precious Leonora, I suppose?"

"What the devil do you mean?"

"Well, it isn't quite nice to pay such a lot of attention to another man's wife, with your own wife looking on, is it?"

"Good God, you're not going to pretend that you object to my friendship with Leonora after all this time."

"If it wasn't such a dreadful thing to say, I should ask if it were only friendship."

"Elizabeth, what the hell's the matter with you? You're not going to pretend, that you, of all people, are jealous."

"Why me of all people?" I asked curiously. "Don't I feel the same as other women?"

"You've never behaved like this before, it's as if a stranger was talking through your lips."

I could not help laughing at that.

"Do you like the stranger?" I asked, with a Vera Ambrose glance.

He frowned, and then laughed shortly; he had nice white teeth.

"Elizabeth, what you need is a shaking."

"That's a fairly mild prescription, Mr Buschner wanted to wring my neck."

"I'm not surprised."

"He told me so."

"What—the devil he did—"

"Gerald, must you swear so much?"

It was not that I really minded so much, but I have the habit of trying to stop Tom from using bad words because of the kiddies.

"Oh, do stop play-acting," he looked at me intently. "You've been unlike yourself lately, don't you feel well?"

"I am quite well."

"Well then, for the Lord's sake, behave like a human being, and don't be later for dinner than you can help."

He left the room.

Late for dinner indeed. Whose fault would that be?

A knock on the door; the maid, Foley, came in and told me that my bath was ready. Should I have time for a bath? Did one have to have one before dinner as well as in the morning? But perhaps Elizabeth took hers at night.

I was conducted to a beautiful bathroom. The walls were done in a shiny sort of blue paint, and there was a frieze of pictures of funny-looking fishes round the top of them. The floor was made of blue tiles, and might have been cold, only there was a cork square with ever such a thick blue bath mat, to stand on. The bath was big and deep, with shining taps, and the water came out of one of them *boiling*. There was a towel-horse made of shiny rails that were really pipes, so hot that you could hardly touch them without burning yourself, and lovely thick soft bath towels. On a glass shelf were large glass jars of different coloured bath salts, and also bottles of different scents.

I felt I could stay there soaking and splashing for ever; and thought how different it was from the bath at home, with the chipped enamel inside, so that one has to be careful where one sits, the faded linoleum on the floor, and the water that runs so slowly and is so often tepid.

A gong sounded while I was still in my bath, so I scurried out of it, thinking how late I should be.

Foley was waiting for me in the bedroom to help me to dress; she always made me a little shy, as she seemed such a refined person. She didn't give me any woollies to put on, but of course the house was so warm that I should not need them, but there were very nice pink undies with lots of real lace, lovely thin stockings, and black shoes with fascinating shiny buckles.

Foley put me into an evening dress made of black velvet that showed a lot of back. It seemed rather plain to me, I looked very slim and straight in it. She then opened a big jewel case in which there were several tiers. I thought it looked like a real treasure chest, when I saw brooches and necklaces, bracelets, ear-rings and rings, all in velvet compartments. I just stared. Late for dinner or not I had no intention of hurrying over my choice. I took a sort of collar of emeralds and diamonds, and put it round my neck; it looked wonderful. Then I found some emerald and diamond ear-rings, long ones, and some bangles; I put on two or three of these and a big diamond brooch like a spray, that cheered up the dress a lot.

Then I saw the pearls—three long ropes of them—and one shorter one. I put the ropes on and looked happily at my reflection in the mirror.

"I think I want something on my head now," said I, wondering if it was a grand enough party for a tiara.

Foley, who had been looking rather stunned, smiled respectfully as though I had made a joke. I gathered that it was not a tiara occasion.

I selected another very pretty brooch, pinned it on my shoulder and told Foley that she might close the case now. She looked as though she did not quite understand what I meant, and stared at me as I sailed out of the room.

I made my way downstairs, and found what seemed to me to be a tremendous collection of people. I learned later that a good many of them had come from other houses to dine.

There was a clatter of talk, some people were drinking cocktails. Several strangers greeted me, and I noticed that they looked at me rather hard. I hoped they were admiring my appearance.

There was a cheer when the thin woman arrived; someone said: "Bravo, Dora, only half-an-hour behind time."

"The Duchess is generally late isn't she?" asked a man who stood near me.

So Dora was a Duchess. I determined to have a good look at her. I wondered if she was the Dora of whom I had already heard, who owned the musical horse.

It was decided not to wait for Leonora, who came in while we were at dinner. I sat between two strange men. There were little cards with people's names on them in front of every place. I managed to find out that my two neighbours were labelled, 'Captain Curff' and 'Lord Ardale.'

Mr Buschner was opposite me at dinner, and looked at me often. Leonora sat on one side of him, when at length she arrived. She called across the table to me:

"You've got 'em all on to-night, Elizabeth. Are you disguised as a Christmas tree?"

"What's the good of having jewels, if you don't wear them?" I asked.

"So you seem to think," she laughed.

She herself only had on a long string of things that looked like dark reddish beads, though I think they were really made of some sort of stone. Her dress was the colour of old gold, made of some crinkly shiny stuff, high up to the neck in front, opening on her chest, and with no back to it at all.

The dinner proceeded. I tasted caviare for the first time in my life, only having seen it in shop windows until then. I thought it was like cold jellied semolina soaked in sea water. One mouthful was enough. I took a gulp of something that looked like water, which they had given to me in a little glass, and was nearly choked, it burned so.

"What is it?" I gasped.

"What—the vodka?" said Captain Curff. "Don't you like it with caviare?"

"It's very burny," I said with tears in my eyes.

Captain Curff asked me what sport we had been having in our part of the world. I told him brightly that we had shot ever so many, and then discovered that he was talking about hunting foxes. We floundered along for a time, until I thought of asking him to tell me what he had been doing lately, after which I was able to eat some of the very good dinner in peace. I think he found me stupid, as I misunderstood him so often.

I began the conversation with my other neighbour by asking him how long it had taken him to get here to-night, and then found that he was staying in the house. To cover up that slip I talked hastily about the house itself, and asked if he did not think it both pretty and comfortable. He said he had always thought so.

"I wonder how the Marquis of Avon likes letting it," said I, determined to be in the know about something.

"Father finds the rent useful in these hard times," replied Lord Ardale.

"Good gracious, are you the Marquis' son?"

"I've—I've always believed so." The young man looked at me with wide open eyes. I blushed. He asked, "Do tell me, Lady Elizabeth, is it a game?"

"Is what a game?"

"Are you trying to make me say a special word, or do you want me to pretend we've never met before, or something?"

"Oh, no—of course not—I'm afraid I'm a little absent-minded sometimes."

He seemed to suspect me of making fun of him. Altogether I was not a great success with either of my dinner companions.

After dinner, when the ladies had gone into the drawing room, leaving the gentlemen behind, I thought again longingly of home. They would now be playing games there, I supposed.

"A penny for your thoughts, darling." Leonora's voice sounded quite close to me.

"I was thinking how little it feels like Christmas here." It was true. There was holly in the house, great boughs of it, but not hung up or stuck behind the pictures in the proper Christmas way, and though we had eaten turkey, it was with cranberry sauce. There had indeed been crackers on the dinner table, but not the usual kind, only some that looked like flowers and had little ornaments inside; none of the women had put on caps, and only very few of the men, and there were no children about.

"Yes, thank God, Emmeline manages to avoid the Christmas atmosphere," said Leonora.

"And isn't it frightful?" Now spoke the Duchess. "I used to suffer from it terribly when Arthur was alive; we had Christmas trees and tenants' balls, and every horror, at Harlesden."

"Giles has a Christmas complex," said Leonora. "So I always let him take the boys down to Whippingford, to the grandparents."

"Have you got boys?" I stared at her.

"Darling, what are you talking about?"

"I forgot for the moment." I felt myself blushing, and decided that I must be more careful to think before I spoke.

"So does Leonora," chuckled the Duchess.

"Whenever I can; children are the biggest bores on earth. You're lucky, Elizabeth," said Leonora.

So Elizabeth had no children, probably did not want them—yet she had played for hours with mine.

Emmeline joined our group, and asked:

"What are you all discussing?"

"We were saying how marvellously you preserve us from the Christmas feeling," said Dora, who seemed pleased, for some reason, at the interruption.

"Bellows and I can't stand it," said Emmeline.

"We ought to form an Anti-Christmas League," said Leonora.

"You needn't ask me to join," I said.

"Why, Elizabeth, you don't care for that sort of thing!" exclaimed Mrs Darnelton.

I felt indignant and, almost forgetting my borrowed personality, told them what I thought. I quoted Tom a good deal as I gave them my views; talked about the meaning of Christmas, and the friendly feeling it gave people to know that hundreds and millions of families were joining in a common celebration all over the world; spoke of how children looked forward to it, and what fun it was giving them surprises,—then I remembered that Elizabeth had no children,—and stopped short.

There was silence from my audience for a moment or so, then Leonora said:

"Did you learn all that out of a book, darling, or are you going on the stage?"

Just then the gentlemen came in, and Bellows, who seemed in very good spirits, came up to us clamouring and requesting that we should go into the Music Room and dance.

"You don't know what you've missed," said Leonora. "Elizabeth has been giving us a Dickens lecture on the wonders of the festive season."

"Oh, how marvellous! Do go on Lady Elizabeth," piped Mr Hardleigh.

"I wasn't joking," I told him curtly.

Emmeline seemed anxious to change the subject, and seconded her husband's proposal that we should dance. I did not feel very much like dancing, as I was afraid that I might be rather out of practice, as Tom and I do very little of that sort of thing these days; but I went with the others into the big room where Mr Buschner had played.

They turned on a very large gramophone called a Panatrope, which played very loudly, and began to dance. Some of them, I should have thought, were rather old for this amusement, but that did not seem to occur to anybody. Several gentlemen asked me to dance but I refused, thinking that I should prefer to look on.

Colonel Massey sat on a sofa beside me, and told me a long story, about bridge I think, though I do not really remember. Watching the dancing was amusing. Emmeline Darnelton and her husband both performed very well, especially Bellows, in spite of his being rather fat. Leonora glided as though she had no bones at all, and I thought Gerald moved very easily.

Mr Buschner approached me, wanted me to come away from the noise, and talk to him somewhere quietly. I refused, as I did not want another argument with him. The music was beginning to fascinate me, an inclination to dance crept into my limbs. In one of the pauses, while someone was putting new tunes on the gramophone, Emmeline and Gerald stood by the sofa where I was.

"Do come and dance, Elizabeth," she said. "It's such wonderful exercise."

A partner grabbed her as the music started again, and she whirled on to the floor.

"Feeling too tired?" asked Gerald.

"I might not be if you were very pressing."

I looked up at him, smiling.

He raised his eyebrows, one higher than the other.

"Come on then." He pulled me off the sofa, and we started dancing. I am only a fair dancer, but I did my best to follow him, mentally counting my steps. I stumbled a little at first, but found it easier later.

In a strange way I felt as if my body knew how to dance, though my mind could not direct it properly, as if a novice driver were at the wheel of a very good car. I realised that Elizabeth's muscles were more supple than mine, and wondered if she could direct my body to do things to which my mind was not accustomed.

Gerald held me exactly right, and steered well. Tom usually grips his partner, and bounces over the ground. I could feel how strong Major Forrester was, though he held me so lightly.

In spite of my annoyance at being where I was on this particular day, I enjoyed myself, and cried "That was fine," when the tune stopped, smiling at Gerald quite naturally as if he had been Tom. He laughed; he had a pleasant laugh and his eyes crinkled attractively at their corners.

"Come and have a drink. It's damned hot in here."

We went into another room, some little way off, where there was a large table covered with glasses, jugs, decanters, and sandwiches of all kinds. I chose some orangeade, and he helped himself to a whisky and soda.

"You weren't up to your usual form, were you?" he asked.

"Wasn't I—anyway I enjoyed it."

"You're in a funny mood to-night, Elizabeth."

"Haven't I behaved myself like a human being?"

Abruptly he said: "I like that dress of yours in spite of the chandelier effect. It suits you." His voice was friendly, and his eyes looked as if they liked what they saw.

"Am I too dazzling?" I asked, innocently.

He laughed again. "How much nicer you look when you're not frowning," I said suddenly.

He came and put his hands on my shoulders; though warm they were not in the least damp, even after all that dancing. "Elizabeth, what's made you so unlike yourself?"

"Don't I generally notice your expression?"

His dark eyes looked straight into mine. They are brown with deep lights in them.

"It doesn't generally seem to interest you much."

My heart began to beat.

Ought I to be letting him touch me like this? I could not help thinking him attractive; but he was a married man, I was Tom's wife, even though camouflaged in someone else's skin—I could have moved away, but I did not want to bring the cold cross look back to his face—not just yet.

"Do you really think that?" The words came of themselves.

His voice grew softer; it is deep and has a sort of vibration in it.

"Are you telling me that you are going to be kinder to me, Eliza?"

I did not quite know what to say next.

His eyes made me feel shy. I looked at his thick brown moustache and—just then a voice drawled: "What a touching domestic scene."

Gerald and I turned and faced Leonora and Mr Buschner. Leonora was laughing, but she did not seem pleased. Mr Buschner looked serious. "Finished dancing?" asked Gerald calmly.

"It's getting too hot up there, even Emmeline is contemplating opening a window. I found Buschner suffering from dance music, and rescued him."

"Have a drink," proposed Gerald.

"Some of the others are going to play Poker—are you going to join them, Gerald?" continued Lady Giles.

"I don't think so, isn't it getting rather late?"

"I expect you're right. Somehow I don't think it would be a lucky evening for you at cards."

She looked very pretty as she sat balanced on the arm of a sofa, holding her glass. I could not help admiring her, but I felt that had I been the real Elizabeth I should have wanted to smack her face.

"I am sure Forrester is lucky at most things," said Mr Buschner heavily.

"It's a question of what you call luck," said Gerald, lighting a cigarette.

"You've nothing to grumble at, Buschner, you're world famous," said Leonora.

"Perhaps that is due more to genius and hard work than luck," I put in politely.

I was feeling kinder now and sorry that I had hurt his feelings. Of course, it was wrong of him to make love to me, but he did look unhappy. I smiled at him, but he did not smile back.

Emmeline now appeared with a good many other people, and there was a buzz of chatter. Suddenly I felt very tired. It had been a long day.

I slipped behind some of the crowd and manoeuvred myself into a big chair at the end of the room. Still more people had arrived and were talking and drinking and laughing. Major Curff was talking to Gerald. I shut my eyes and thought of home; the blessed feeling for which I had been longing came over me, and in a moment I was back where I wanted to be.

XI

I had returned to an agitated home. When I came to myself I was in our sitting room, sitting by the fire smoking a cigarette. The furniture had all been pushed back. I could hear Tom locking up outside; it was nearly one o'clock.

When he came in I heard something of the doings of Elizabeth.

"Good Lord, Polly, you aren't smoking again?"

I threw the cigarette away, hating the taste of it in my mouth.

"Oh, I just thought I would try it."

"You've been trying a good many things this evening, I can't make you out."

"Never mind making me out, give me a kiss old boy."

I felt so pleased to see him.

"Very affectionate to me all of a sudden, aren't you, after keeping me at arm's length all the evening and carrying on with Syd and Jack."

"I—carried on?"

"Well you danced with Jack, didn't you, and gassed away to Syd about all sorts of musical blokes with foreign names I never knew you'd heard of, till Ethel got quite sniffy."

I gaped.

Dancing! So that's why the room was cleared.

"Didn't you enjoy the dancing?" I queried.

"Oh—perhaps—for a bit, but I didn't like Aunt Abigail leaving early in a huff."

Before we went to bed I gathered more information about what had happened in my spiritual absence. Elizabeth, disguised as me, had talked quite a lot about books, music and pictures, and "fairly woken up Syd"; had stopped one of Tom's favourite records because it was a little scratched, and had played the piano, causing universal astonishment, saying that she had not altogether forgotten what she had learnt at school. Well, I had been taught the piano at school, but had never been any good. Mentally I cursed her, still I had committed her to playing bridge, which was a satisfactory thing to remember.

My understudy had spent ages putting the kids to bed, cut short the Christmas games after supper, and had ended by pushing back the furniture and making everybody, except Aunt Abigail, dance, even Cousin Fanny.

"Don't you think Cousin Fanny enjoyed it?" I enquired, breathless with curiosity.

"Aunt Abigail didn't; she's never left early on Christmas night before. You'll have to go and smooth her down."

"Do you think I was rude to her?" I asked, with distinctly kinder feelings towards my substitute.

"No—well not exactly, but where on earth did you pick up that superior way of talking?"

"Perhaps from the Talkies," I giggled.

"Well, don't copy any more of the same kind," said Tom, adding suddenly, "and what in thunder made you forget to kiss old Abbie and Fanny good-bye?"

"Absence of mind, I suppose, dearie."

"You were like another person, I can't think why you went on like that. It wasn't funny."

"Wasn't it?" I said feebly.

Then suddenly I was very sorry for Tom, and furious with Elizabeth for spoiling his Christmas like that. I wanted a chance to get even with her.

"Tommy boy, I'm sorry, I never meant to spoil your fun," I said with perfect sincerity.

It was some time before I could bring back his good humour. During the next few days I experienced more results of Elizabeth's visit to my house. One trace of her activities I discovered in our bedroom; she had removed Tom's brushes and combs off the dressing table, and put them on a little table in the bathroom under the window, where his shaving mirror hangs.

Though I was furious with her for meddling, and Tom annoyed, we did both keep to the new arrangement in the end, as it was more comfortable. My own brushes and so on, of which I've quite a nice imitation ivory set, with my initials in silver on the back, looked much more important neatly set out. She had also put my powder and puff into a box that I had been keeping on the mantelpiece as an ornament, and placed it in front of my looking glass.

Other effects of her presence reacted from the family. Ethel was distinctly haughty with me, and asked me since when I had become a vamp. She was also very curious to know where I had learnt to play the piano. I murmured something about practising in my spare time.

"Spare time," she snorted. "You always said you never had enough time to get through everything you were obliged to do."

She took a lot of coaxing before she would be friendly again, and was upset at once when Syd, who came to call for her, wanted me to go to a concert with him. I refused that invitation energetically, and had a good deal of trouble in convincing him that I had only been pulling his leg when I had talked to him so much about music.

"You did it very well, I could have sworn that you knew what you were talking about," he said, looking curiously at me.

The only thing that made Ethel smile again was the memory of Aunt Abigail's displeasure.

"I didn't know you had the gumption to put the old girl in her place like that," she said.

"Oh, did you think I was rude to her?"

"No, not rude, but somehow you treated her quite civilly, as though she didn't really matter."

Sydney laughed. "I wish you would teach me how to disagree with people and be smiling and polite all the time. She didn't know where she was."

Soon afterwards I visited Aunt Abigail, and found her distinctly less aggressive than usual. She talked plaintively about her age and how little young people heeded their elders in these days. It was just as trying as her crushing moods. She complained that Fanny had been suffering from rheumatism, no doubt brought on by catching cold after dancing on Christmas night.

Fanny, to my surprise, denied this hotly.

"You'd no business to dance at your age, it was a shame to make you. You'll be forty-three next birthday," deplored the aunt.

I thought of Dora at Thinnesley, who was certainly older than that, and had danced merrily all night.

"Forty is young in these days," I pronounced. "Especially if you don't look it."

Cousin Fanny actually smiled amiably at me and told me that she had enjoyed herself and had bought some face powder of the kind that I had recommended to her. It was very surprising.

I did not mind what Elizabeth had done to Abigail and Fanny, but she had made the children difficult to manage. They kept on wanting more stories about Drinlaw Castle and the ogre who lived there, and the stag of Kirrie Glen, and more games like those they had played after the Christmas tree. Cinderella and the Three Bears had lost their charm.

Tom was not happy either. He referred at times to things I had said and done, which he did not like, and was quite annoyed when Jack Sparlow tried to urge us to come to a Subscription Dance.

"We are not gad-abouts," said Tom.

"But when a lady dances like Mrs Tom, it's a shame for her not to do it more," said Mr Sparlow.

Tom refused absolutely and seemed to have fixed it in his head that I had encouraged Sparlow to flirt with me. It transpired that I had called him 'Jack,' which he wanted me to go on doing. One day he invited me to go to the pictures with him on a Saturday afternoon when Tom would be watching football.

I have never made a habit of going out without Tom, and told Jack Sparlow so, but I could not be cross with him for wanting to take me out.

"There'd be no great harm in it," he said. "I thought you might like a bit of fun sometimes."

"Why—surely I never led you to suppose—"

"Well—you did call me 'Jack' and asked me to dance with you."

"Oh—that was just because it was Christmas and you're a friend of Tom's."

"I'd like to be a friend of yours too."

"You're no friend to either of us if you can't behave yourself," I told him. He left after that.

I wondered if Elizabeth was a fast woman. Mr Buschner had accused her of appearing aloof, or remote, or something. She did not appear to have been so with Syd and Sparlow. I hated her for making Tom believe that I was a flighty kind of person. I was not. There had been that episode with Gerald of course—but that was different somehow—it was not really me—or not altogether.

Mr Marshall called in the middle of my reflections. He always thinks that, because he was a friend of Dad's, we can never be anything but glad to see him. He came in, slowly and heavily as usual, and took my hand in both of his. I had felt that he would pat me on the head in another minute.

"How's little Polly to-day?" he began. "Busy about the household tasks, I suppose. Don't make company of me, my dear."

He sat down on the smallest chair in the room and clasped his hands on his tummy. I knew he had come to stay. The room felt smaller with Mr Marshall in it.

I have always been fond of our home and all our things, but it had struck me during the last few days that the rooms were too small and too full. I had this feeling very strongly as I contemplated the visitor.

My intention had been to take a breath of air before the children came back from Winnie Rayne's birthday party, but to move would have offended Mr Marshall, so I found some sewing and worked while he talked. He told me all about his dog, Claribel, and her puppies, and stories of her great intelligence, most of which I had heard before. The worst of Mr Marshall is that, every ten minutes or so, he expects an answer so that one is obliged to listen to him.

"Ah, my dear Polly, you do not know the comfort a dog can be to a lonely old man."

"Nonsense, you're not old, Mr Marshall."

"I know better, alas, my child, but I always say that every age has its compensations. When the flame of youth burns out, there is a warm and comfortable glow in the red embers of middle age. There are the pleasures of memory, pictures in the fire. Youth is spent in making the pictures, that age may enjoy the pleasures of contemplating them."

"The pleasant ones, I hope," said I, biting off a thread.

"Ah, yes, indeed," he sighed, "Yes, some of the pleasing ones bring sad memories; still, the softening influence of time turns keen sorrow to gentle melancholy." He shook his head, sighing again, and I knew he was thinking of Letitia Davies, who jilted him and married somebody else, thirty years ago.

It seemed a very long time till Millie Rayne brought the children back. It is always difficult to get the children to be polite to Mr Marshall, but I managed to make them shake hands with him; and they did not remain unduly grave when he joked about the pains they would get from eating plum cake at the party. When he told them, however, that holding a guinea pig up by the tail causes its eyes to drop out, Bobby quite politely told him that somebody must have been taking him in, because guinea pigs have no tails, and I then decided that it was bed time.

I got Mr Marshall to amuse himself with the wireless while I put the kids to bed, and did not hurry back to him. I found him eventually listening to a dance band, and begged him not to turn it off, but he did, saying, "Voices from the air, my child. Such things were not known in my time. I am not sure that I care for such new-fangled things. I like to sit quietly by my fireside and hear the homely voice of a friend."

Tom's face fell when he came home and saw our guest; he wanted to talk to me about football, but got no chance to do so, for Mr Marshall, after saying, "Ah, sport in the open air, nothing like it for young limbs," went on to explain what a good game cricket was, and to tell many anecdotes of matches played long ago. He stayed to tea and supper, and shook us warmly by the hand when he left.

"You children are good for an old fellow; the talk of the young renews youth," he said. Which was hardly to the point as the talk had mainly consisted of a monologue by himself.

"Damn the man," said Tom when the door closed behind Marshall. "Couldn't you pretend to be dead the next time he comes, Pollikins?" He yawned as if his jaw would break.

I wondered what Elizabeth would do with Mr Marshall. She certainly would not be able to get him to dance with her.

Next day I saw in the papers a picture of the Hon. Phyllis Brent, who was engaged to Mr Anthony Launde. It was Phyllis. I did so hope Mr Anthony Launde was Toby. I felt I should like to write and congratulate them.

I found out all about her in the gossip column. She was the second daughter of Lord Windlesham, the peer who was so much interested in fishing, and Toby was the third son of Colonel Walter Launde of somewhere or other, and brother to the celebrated gentleman rider. I read in the same paper that Lady Giles Gilray had left for St. Moritz, and wondered if Gerald had gone as well.

It suddenly struck me how dreadful it would be if Elizabeth should take it into her mind to whisk me off to a foreign country, where I should not be able to speak the language. It was a great relief to read a few days later that Major and Lady Elizabeth Forrester had entertained a party for the Wellborough Hunt Ball. There was a list of guests; the only names in it familiar to me were those of Phyllis and, as I hoped, Toby.

I reflected that I should not have minded going to the Hunt Ball, but Elizabeth had evidently decided to keep that pleasure for herself.

It was nearly the end of January before our next game of General Post was played. A foggy morning dawned, and everything in my neighbourhood seemed to go wrong. The new girl who had come last Christmas time quarrelled with Gladys, and both threatened to give notice. Something went wrong with the boiler and there was no hot bath water. Bobby started a cold, and Tom lost a collar stud and went off, late, to the office in a very bad temper. I thought longingly of my other life, and how perhaps the sun would be shining in the country and Elizabeth taking the dogs for a walk before luncheon.

I shut my eyes, really glad to feel swimmy ... but I opened them very suddenly, for I found myself sitting on the back of a horse!

XII

I looked down in horror. The ground seemed a terrible long way down. I have never ridden except at the seaside, on a donkey, and did not know in the least what was going to happen. No doubt Elizabeth's body was accustomed to riding, but could it keep me in the saddle without the direction of her mind? If I had not been so frightened I should have thought the scene pretty. There was no sun, but ever so many scarlet coats, worn by men on horseback, seemed to fill the landscape with colour. My horse and I were standing in a very green field near to a wood. Of course, there were no leaves on the trees, but there seemed to be a good deal of green in the undergrowth, and here and there were evergreens. From the wood came the voice of a man uttering strange cries, and now and then the crack of a whip.

I wondered what I had better do next. I longed to get off, but dared not move for fear of upsetting the horse, which was standing quite still. My boots were splashed with mud, and my hands seemed to be full of reins. It was difficult to hold them and a whip as well. Frantically I wished myself back home, sending desperate mental S.O.S.'s to my other self, but without avail.

The voice of the man in the wood got further away. People who had been standing still began to move on. My horse went too, making my heart jump, but he only walked quite slowly beside the wood, behind the horse in front. I could hear people talking behind me, but dared not look round. I held the reins as I had found them, not daring to pull them. To my great relief the walking pace of my steed was rather pleasant. I hoped it would go on; but I had a horrible conviction that the beast would soon begin to run, and then where should I be!

The apprehension was correct. There came a yelping noise from somewhere among the trees. A quiver ran right through the body of the animal between my knees. His ears went forward, his head up. I wondered if now was the time to jump off, but was afraid of getting kicked, as more horse riders came near and round us, all looking interestedly forward. I bundled all the reins into my left hand, and with the right took firm hold of a bit of the saddle in front of me. There was much more yelping now, and suddenly another man's voice, at a little distance, called out something that sounded like, "A—a—ay." Then things happened. Voices were saying, "They're away," in pleased tones, and what seemed like a sea of horses swept on in the direction of the sound.

My beast was galloping before I knew where I was. I held on with might and main, feeling as if my teeth were being jerked through the top of my head. The reins seemed to be flapping all over the place. I could not get hold of them properly. I let my whip fall as I could not hold it and grasp the saddle as well. Somewhere I had heard it said that one should grip with one's knees, but it seemed very difficult to do, because my mind was too terrified to trust them. I bumped all over the saddle. There was a sound like thunder as all the horses galloped up a little hill. When we arrived at the top of it, I saw the hounds in front, scudding across the field, like little pied clouds, yelling hard as they ran. A man in red followed them closely, and the rest of our company scurried after him. It was the only one glimpse that I had of all this because my gaze was mostly divided between my horse's head and the saddle.

Mixed up with my fear and discomfort was a strange sort of excitement. I blinked tears out of my eyes as we careered along. The field was a large one, but we seemed to cross it very quickly and long before we got to its other side my hand was aching from my grip of the saddle.

We whirled up to a hedge, and no words can describe my feelings when I realised that people were jumping over it. Luckily for me, somebody opened a gate, and a crowd of us crammed and jammed through it. I was bumped on both sides. And someone said, "Damn you! where are you going?" in my ear. I moaned, "I wish I knew," as we shot into another field.

I was nearly hurled off as my horse swung left, and my feet were jerked out of the stirrups. We flashed like lightning down a hill, right to a hedge with a little ditch in front of it. My horse's front part rose in the air, and I flew like a cricket ball from a bowler's hand, off his back.

There was a moment borrowed from eternity before the ground seemed to hit me all over. I lay where I was until my bewildered senses came slowly back. Someone was bending over me, asking if I was hurt. Cautiously I sat up; except that every one of my nerves was jarred, I did not seem to be damaged, but for a slight ache in one shoulder.

The hounds were now quite out of hearing, though plenty of horses were galloping on after them. Two gentlemen in red and one in a black coat, with a bowler hat, got off their horses, and had come to see to me.

In one of the red coated ones I recognised Captain Champion, in the other the man with grey eyes who had sat next to me at that shooting lunch. To their enquiries I answered that I was not badly hurt, and let Captain Champion pull me up to my feet. One or two people riding by pulled up to ask how I was, and reassured, rode on.

"No bones broken, that's good. Have some of this," said the Captain holding out a thin glass bottle to me.

"No—steady, there may be a touch of concussion," said the other.

The black coated man enquired if my Ladyship was all right now.

"I—I think so."

The grey-eyed man climbed on to his horse.

"Come, Jarvis, see if we can catch that horse," he said, and the black-coated man followed him.

"Take it easy," said Captain Champion, and added. "I can't quite make out what happened to you. I was just behind you at the fence, and saw you had lost both stirrups."

"I can't explain," I said helplessly. Then I looked round the field from which all riders had disappeared. "How do I get away from here?" I wanted to know.

"Oh, they'll have your horse in a moment."

"I'm not going to get on to that horse again, not if I know it."

"Why?" he seemed surprised. "Did Corsair make a mistake?"

"I don't know if he did, I made several," I quavered.

"You've had a nasty shaking," said Champion sympathetically. He looked up as horses thundered towards us. "Here comes Rockley with your horse."

The grey-eyed man was holding my horse by the bridle.

"Here he is, Lady Elizabeth," he announced cheerfully. "I've asked Jarvis to find your second horseman, in case you want him."

When I again declared that nothing would make me get on the horse, because I should certainly fall off if I did, both men seemed rather at a loss. "Are you feeling ill?" asked Rockley.

"No, not really, but I want to go home."

"Where have you sent your car?" enquired Champion.

Naturally I could give them no information about that. They exchanged glances and Rockley, saying something about "finding Forrester," galloped off, leaving me with Captain Champion, who took charge of both his steed and mine. Slowly we walked across the field, which was not easy, in boots, as the ground was squelchy.

Eventually Captain Champion persuaded me to get up on my horse again while he held it. He promised to lead it if I did. Getting up was rather a business, but we managed it somehow, and, though I was nervous when he mounted in his turn, my horse did nothing savage while he held it by the head. He kept his promise, took hold of my reins, and we proceeded at a foot's pace. He was very kind and sympathetic, and as the day was not cold, and the horses went quietly, I began not to mind being on horseback. If it was no worse than that, ever, I thought that I might like riding.

Even though I was so much recovered, my thoughts were extremely bitter about Elizabeth. I wondered if she had planted me on horseback as a revenge for the trouble I might have made for her at Christmas. It seemed to me a cruel thing to have done. Did she mean to hurt me badly? Yet it was *her* body that would have been harmed. I could not understand her.

I was silent while I was thinking all this, but Captain Champion did not let me brood for long. He took such trouble to distract me, that I was laughing when, on turning into a lane, we met Gerald and the man called Rockley.

Gerald looked very nice indeed in his red coat. He seemed vexed and anxious as he rode up to me and enquired how I was feeling. He also thanked Captain Champion for looking after me, and condoled with us both for missing a very good hunt. Then he urged both the others to go on and find the hounds, telling them where they had gone to, and saying that he would take charge of me. After more politeness on both sides, the two gentlemen left me with Gerald.

I told him that both Captain Champion and Mr Rockley had been most kind. His eyebrows went up. "They will feel less kind if they lose a good day," he said. He was leading my horse now, and seemed not to understand why it was necessary. He was eager to know what had happened to me. "Do tell me what the devil came over you, Elizabeth? Rockley informed me that you went at a fence like hell and the night, having lost both stirrups, and were jumped off."

"I couldn't help it."

"But why, were you feeling faint, or what? Did Corsair make a mistake?"

"The only mistake in the story was my being on his back."

"But there must be some reason. You were all right this morning, you look all right now. Surely you don't want me to go on leading the brute?"

"Gerald, if you let him go I shall scream."

He found no answer to that and spoke no more till we got on to a main road where we met the big blue car, which, I subsequently found out, had been telephoned for, and two men on horseback, who I decided were grooms. They had black coats and bowler hats, and leather cases on straps round their waists, and touched their hats to us. The one who came and held my horse's head said something about how sorry he was to hear that my Ladyship had had a fall.

I got down carefully, very pleased to be rid of the horse. The chauffeur was holding a thick coat, lined with fur, ready for me. I waved it aside. "Heavens, I don't want that on top of these thick clothes."

"Good God, put it on and don't catch cold on the top of everything else," said Gerald irritably. Then, as I did what he told me to, he asked me if I wanted him to come home with me.

I was surprised. "You surely wouldn't leave me after I've had a tumble?"

He got off his horse and handed the beast over to the groom.

"Still feeling shaky? A touch of concussion, I expect."

He put on a fur-lined coat too, and got into the car with me. We started on the way to Heringdon.

XIII

We were silent for a time on the way home. My feelings towards Elizabeth were bitter. How cruel it had been of her to place me in such danger. I might have been badly hurt. It crossed my mind that she might not have known that I was no rider.

I studied Gerald's profile after a while; I liked his thick hair and the shape of his chin, which had a cleft in it.

He noticed my scrutiny eventually, and asked me what I was thinking.

"I was thinking how nice you look in hunting kit."

He seemed surprised. "Why all of a sudden?"

"Oh, it just seemed to strike me."

"You must have come a devil of a whack, my dear, to make you start paying me compliments."

"I don't see why I should not say nice things to you, if I want to. Is it forward to admire one's own husband?"

He seemed about to say something, changed his mind and grunted.

There was a further silence. Then he enquired, "Feeling all right?"

"Yes, I was just thinking how much nicer it is riding in a car than on horseback."

His eyebrows went up again.

"What was it made your nerve go like that? Rockley told me that you were all to pieces, and I couldn't believe my eyes when I saw that bounder Champion riding in your pocket."

"Why do you call Captain Champion a bounder? He was very kind to me."

"It looked like it. Still he certainly missed a good hunt on your account, so did Rockley."

"He and Mr Rockley were both kind," I said.

Gerald looked hard at me. "You did have concussion then. I heard that you could not remember where the car was."

"That's quite true," I giggled. "But I don't feel like concussion at all."

However, Gerald was convinced that bed was the only place for me, and he handed me over to the charge of Foley when we arrived. She was full of concern, and got a bath ready. I was always a little bit shy of Miss Foley; she was so very ladylike that it felt odd to be waited on by her.

It seemed strange to be in a bath in the middle of the day, but it was not unpleasant, as I had a good many bruises. There was no escape from bed though it seemed to me a waste of time to go there. I reflected that bed seemed to end most of my visits to Heringdon, and made up my mind to get up as soon as I could. If Elizabeth switched me into her life against my will, at least I would get all the possible fun out of it that I could.

Gerald, now dressed in tweed clothes, came to see me. He was quite polite, but I thought him remiss; Tom would have come and put his arms round me and comforted me.

When I had reassured him about my aches and pains, he moved towards the door. I stopped him.

"Aren't you going to stay and talk to me, Gerald? Tell me all the news. Have you heard from Leonora lately? Is she enjoying St. Moritz?"

He frowned. "You know as much about that as I do."

"Do I?"

"Elizabeth you're not going to start playing the fool again are you?"

"Am I playing the fool?" I looked at him under my lashes.

"You ought to tell Sellyn about these queer moods of yours. There must be something badly wrong with your nerves."

"Why?"

"Well, think of how you behaved at the December shoot, and then at Christmas—"

"Didn't you like me at Christmas?" I said archly.

"You best know what you did then, and why you did it," he said curtly. "And look at you to-day, all to pieces."

"Well, I did have a tumble, didn't I?"

"And you keep on using the most extraordinary phraseology. There must be some explanation of it all."

"Of all what?"

"Of your amazing unlikeness to yourself."

"You do not seem to dislike me when I'm unlike myself." I smiled at him with my head on one side, like Vera Ambrose.

He came nearer and looked down at me. "You're incredibly ghastly when you put on that coy manner, my dear, yet somehow you remind me of the fact that I once believed I had married a woman and not an iceberg."

His tone was quiet, but there was a force of bitterness in it that gave me a shock. I blushed, and could only say:

"Oh!"

"Have you got feelings somewhere, after all, Elizabeth?"

"I expect so," I murmured feebly.

I felt that he meant to be unkind, yet I was sorry for him. He laughed. Not an amused laugh, and went on in the same tone.

"Don't you think you can play with me, my dear. I don't let anyone do that."

Before I could find a possible reply to this, there came a knock on the door and Foley let in the doctor.

"Ah, Sellyn!" Gerald shook hands with him.

"Here's a patient that wants a good bit of vetting. She's been seedy lately."

The doctor said politely regretful things, and Gerald went away leaving me alone with him.

I felt a little nervous; he could hardly find out the real truth, but what conclusion would he come to about me? I decided to be very careful.

Dr Sellyn was long and thin and brown. He wore eye-glasses which looked as though they might fall off at any moment. Before long he had discovered that no bones were broken, and no damage done beyond bruises. He then enquired about my health in general. I answered very warily and told him that I had not been really ill, but that I had been agitated once or twice and that Gerald had got the impression that my nerves were a little out of order.

"Perhaps you have been over-smoking?"

"Would you say that of me?" I said, smiling.

"Most people might," he smiled back. "Try and knock it off as much as you can."

"I shall find no difficulty about that," I answered him.

"H'm, I wonder. It takes determination, doesn't it?"

"Would you say I have a determined character?" I enquired earnestly.

He hesitated. "Yes, I should say you had, if you cared to exercise it. You have always given me the impression that you possess enormous self-control."

"Tell me some more about myself, doctor."

He laughed. "I'm not a fortune-teller, Lady Elizabeth."

"No, of course, but seriously I should like to know what sort of person you think I am."

He seemed puzzled at that, but I explained to him that I had my reasons. I drew from him gradually his opinion.

It seemed to be that I was very sensitive, reserved and highly strung, more so than I allowed anybody to see. That I had not a domineering, or interfering nature. When I asked him if he could imagine my hypnotising someone, he simply laughed at the idea. He left shortly after that, having told me to stay in bed for the day and keep quiet, and said that he would come next morning. He told me to go slow in general, and that he would give me a tonic soon. He thought that my nerves had been over-strained.

"Try not to worry over things too much," had been his parting words, very kindly spoken. I thought that advice impossible to follow.

Who in the world before had ever been in a position like mine! What was she like, the woman who made me do this incredible thing? The doctor did not think her domineering. How had she this complete power over me? He did not think her interfering; but she had made my family and friends dance to her tune.

Mr Buschner had called her aloof and remote. Gerald said she was an iceberg. She had hardly given that impression to Tom, Syd and Mr Sparlow.

Did she take a holiday from her usual behaviour when she changed places with me? What were her feelings about Gerald? Was she fond of him? I thought I could understand it if she were. He seemed to get annoyed with her a good deal, and yet—

What did he mean by my "extraordinary phraseology?" Did I not talk in exactly the same way as everybody else? I decided to get up and see what entertainment Heringdon could provide; but before I could succeed in my design, Foley appeared with a tray. Well, it seemed a pity not to eat lunch as it was there. After that Foley brought a bottle of embrocation and rubbed all my bruises. She seemed to expect me to settle down and go to sleep. That was not my idea. I was not going to waste the resources of Heringdon on staying in bed.

As soon as she had left the room I got out of bed and put on a white velvet dressing gown lined with oyster coloured satin, that looked to me rather like an evening cloak, slipped my feet into soft white slippers without heels, and looked round to see what I could find.

There were books of course, but they did not look any more interesting than the ones in the boudoir. All of a sudden I saw some letters lying open on a table.

Of course one does not read other people's letters, but was not this case exceptional; while I was enveloped in Elizabeth's personality, could I not claim the right to a full use of her possessions? If she placed me in awkward situations, was it not justifiable to cope with them by any means in my power? Her correspondence might tell me something about her.

I glanced through a couple of invitations, and was not greatly interested in a bookseller's list; I found a letter from some friend telling her where to get a particular plant, and mentioning the long Latin names of several varieties. An author wrote answering a letter she appeared to have written thanking him for sending her his new book; he said that some criticism or other she had made was quite just, and wondered how she knew so much about suburban conditions.

How indeed!

Another letter was signed "your affectionate Father." It was long and said a good deal about dogs and horses which were mentioned by name, and gave an account of the making of a new rose garden; but one part of it interested me very much—"No, I have never heard that any of our family were telepathic or hypnotic subjects, or ever had psychic experiences of any kind; I never heard of one who even indulged in second sight. Why are you so anxious to know? If you are interested in things like that, your new neighbour, Arthur Rockley, is a bit of an expert about them, I believe. Personally, the subject has always bored me, and I always thought that it did you too."

I wondered since when the subject had ceased to bore her. Had she kept her experiments a secret from everyone, had there ever been any beside the one that had involved me?

I found another sentence that interested me in an epistle from some woman at St. Moritz, which contained a good deal of information about all sorts of people, mostly referred to by nicknames. This ran: "Leonora is at the Palace, in great form. She never leaves Archie Winstanley. She told me that she had met you and Gerald staying at Thinnesley for Christmas, but was a bit severe about both of you. Was there a row?"

I felt that I too would like to know that.

Foley broke in on my reflections, seeming surprised and pained to find me out of bed, but after some difficulty I persuaded her to give me some outdoor clothes, and I escaped, went downstairs and out into the garden, which I explored.

It was not a good time of the year for flowers, but I enjoyed looking at the terraces and yew hedges, with little bushes cut into funny shapes. I liked the kitchen garden too, and the greenhouses, with all the flowers in them.

Every time I saw a gardener, I went the other way, and avoided conversation; conversations in this second existence so often got complicated. However Gerald and the dogs discovered me in the garden. The dogs ran joyfully up to me and then stopped short. They did not growl, but remained aloof, a little suspiciously.

Gerald was not pleased with me for getting up and tried to persuade me to go back to bed. He told me that Dr Sellyn had found me rather seedy, and recommended my seeing some big-wig doctor in London. I told him gaily that, whatever Dr Sellyn thought, I felt perfectly well, if still rather bruised, and cheerfully enquired how he was going to amuse me. He suggested some sense and a rest. I pouted, "Do you want to get rid of me?"

He seemed puzzled and worried and at a loss what to do next. We returned to the house and, of all curious coincidences, the butler came in and announced, "Lord and Lady Rockley."

The grey-eyed man I had met that morning appeared, accompanied by a pleasant looking woman, dressed in a riding habit and wearing a top hat.

XIV

The visitors shook hands, and said that, as the hounds had killed somewhere or other nearby, they had telephoned for their car to come and pick them up and had called to enquire after me.

I reassured them as to my well-being, and Gerald, after a moment's hesitation, asked them to have some tea. I divined that I should have done this.

They accepted, and Lady Rockley asked if she could come upstairs and repair the ravages caused by the chase. I escorted her to my bedroom.

She seemed very agreeable and told me how much she and her husband liked the neighbourhood. She mentioned places and people, and my answers were rather vague. I noticed that she looked at me in rather a puzzled way once or twice, but I was getting used to this on my excursions into Elizabeth's world.

We rejoined the gentlemen, who were having tea in the hall. There were poached eggs. Gerald talked to Lady Rockley about things the hounds had been doing, while her husband came and sat next to me. He was nice and easy to talk to, but after a time I got the impression that he was studying me. It made me a little uncomfortable; I knew I was floundering. Remembering what Elizabeth's father had said in his letter, I brought the conversation round to telepathy and hypnotism; he asked me if I was interested in mental phenomena.

Lady Rockley's voice broke in: "Do I hear Arthur talking psychics? It's his pet subject, don't let him bore you."

"Psychics? Spooks and that sort of thing," said Gerald.

"I know nothing about spooks," I said, hastily. This is not quite true; I have heard and read many ghost stories, but they frighten me, and I did not want to think about them in a strange house.

"I don't think anybody knows much about spooks," said Lord Rockley. "It is not so much spiritualism that interests me as the curious functioning of the human brain. Cases of aphasia, delusions, hypnotic control and so on. Dr Caument, in Paris, has a very interesting case under observation now. It is one of dual personality."

Gerald, who was lighting a cigarette, looked up quickly. His eyes met mine. "Tell us about it," I asked.

He did.

It appeared that "the case" was a young girl who seemed at intervals to be two totally different people, one called 'Jeanne,' who was gentle and charming, kind, and rather stupid, the other 'Louise,' who was the reverse. 'Jeanne' was very slow at all kinds of learning and quite incapable of doing arithmetic. 'Louise' on the contrary, was very quick, especially at figures.

Curiously enough 'Jeanne' entirely forgot what she had done as 'Louise' and *vice versa*.

"What causes such a condition?" queried Gerald.

"There's no absolute certainty about that yet," replied Rockley. "Hypnotic treatment is generally the cure."

"In mediaeval times such happenings would have been accounted for by diabolical possession. Your friend 'Jeanne-Louise' would have had a thin time in the middle ages," said Lady Rockley laughing.

Soon after that they left, first saying polite things about my recovery from the accident, then asking us to come over to Cottesborough one day soon.

"That would be very nice," I said, "and you must tell me some more about those queer people your doctor friend studies, Lord Rockley."

He laughed and said he could tell me lots more if I was interested, while Lady Rockley smilingly warned me against encouraging him too much to bore me with psychopathic lectures.

When they had gone Gerald looked thoughtfully at me.

"That was a queer thing Rockley told us," he said.

"He told us several."

"Have you got a dual personality, Eliza?" he enquired suddenly.

I jumped. "Gerald, what an idea!"

"You can't deny that you've had moods lately which were like another person altogether."

"Which of the two people do you prefer?" I asked with my head on one side.

He did not smile. "I suppose you do it for a joke; but I don't think it's a very good one," he said gravely.

Before I could find an answer to that, Burke came in saying that somebody wanted to talk to Gerald, who then left the room.

I sat down and began to wonder what would happen next. Gerald had found out that there was a difference between Elizabeth and me. Would he insist on my seeing a doctor? Well, if he did, I should probably be at home by then, unless Elizabeth chose to make me cope with that difficulty. What could any doctor do about a case like ours? Would anyone believe my story if I told it?

I knew that Gerald was anxious about me, or rather Elizabeth; did that mean he liked her? Did Elizabeth like him? He interested me. I wondered if Tom interested her. She did not appear to have been particularly nice to him so far.

Then I began to try and think of my home and will myself back again. In vain.

The prospect of having to spend the night at Heringdon alarmed me. I should be alone with Gerald. Still less did I enjoy the idea of Elizabeth spending the night with Tom. The hussy, would she dare? If she were a fast woman there was nothing she might not do! My Tom—

Gerald's entrance into the room interrupted my reflections. He asked me how I was feeling and being reassured as to my well-being, suggested that it was time we should dress for dinner.

"Good Heavens—think of dinner after that tea!" I cried.

"I wondered why you ate those eggs," he said. "I suppose you had no lunch."

I avoided answering that, and asked: "Are people coming to dine?"

"My dear, what are you talking about? Of course not, are you still feeling muzzy?"

"I just forgot." Then I suggested that he might take me to the pictures. He treated that as a pure joke, and we went upstairs to dress.

Foley appeared in due course, and seemed to expect me to have another bath. Subsequently she helped me into some evening clothes.

I was a little nervous about the intimate dinner with Gerald. Much as I should have liked to make trouble for Elizabeth, I dared not appear too different from what she usually was, in case I got put into an asylum. She might leave me there and live my life at home. So much of what I did and said quite naturally seemed to be unnatural for her.

When we were at table, being waited on by the butler and a footman, as if it was a party, I steered the conversation to plays and films, and allowed Gerald to do most of the talking. Tom and I do not often go to the theatre, but I had seen enough in the newspapers to carry on the talk intelligently for a time.

After dinner we went to the library, where my companion seemed to expect me to read a book. He took one up himself. That appeared to me too dull a way of spending the evening, and I enquired if there was anything good on the wireless. That seemed to surprise him, but he looked up the broadcasting, and said that Buschner was giving a recital in Prague.

With memories of the queer noises he had produced from the piano at Thinnesley, I was on the point of suggesting the vaudeville, or the dance music instead, but checked myself, rather than appear out of character, and listened silently to the strange sounds that made themselves heard when Gerald switched on the set.

When it was over at last, Gerald said, "He can play, that chap. Do you remember that thing he played at Holbourne?" He hummed something.

"Oh yes!" I answered at random.

"Come upstairs and play it to me, Eliza."

Of course, I couldn't do that, and had to say I was tired. He then suggested bed, and I had no reason for refusing to go upstairs.

I found Foley waiting for me with some decoction that the doctor had ordered. She did not leave me until I was in bed. I felt helpless and irritated, and rather frightened, but remembered hopefully that Gerald, unlike Tom, had a room of his own.

Naturally I did not feel sleepy. There was no prospect of escape; Elizabeth's books never appealed to me. I should have liked to inspect some of her clothes, but did not know how to find them. After what seemed like ages, there came a soft knock at the door between Gerald's room and mine. I was dumb. He came quietly in, still in his evening clothes, I was glad to see.

"Are you asleep, Elizabeth?"

"No—but very tired," I said nervously.

He came and sat down on the edge of the bed. This time I did not send him away.

"You look a bit white."

"Oh, I shall be all right after a sleep."

He smiled suddenly. "It's a funny thing to say, but at the moment you actually look rather pathetic."

"I feel rather pathetic," I said meekly.

He leaned towards me and put one of his hands on mine. "Do you really, my sweet?"

I knew that I ought to take my hand away. I knew that Tom was the only man in the world for me, but ... Gerald was pleasant to look at, his deep voice was thrilling when he spoke gently, and curiosity was strong in me. He seemed to be much nearer to me suddenly, and before I expected it, his arm was round my shoulders.

My heart beat very hard. I shivered a little.

"Are you cold?"

His voice was very low, his face very near to mine. Then his arms held me tight, and I felt his moustache on my lips. I was suddenly frightened and pushed him away.

"No ... No ..." I cried.

He let me go and drew back, frowning.

"Do you absolutely hate me?" he asked bitterly.

"Oh, no." I did not hate him. I was trembling all over. "It isn't that, only ... I'm tired ... I've got a bad headache. ... Please, Gerald." My voice quavered a little. I think he saw that I was genuinely upset, because he stopped frowning. He got up from the bed.

"All right, my dear. Of course, you must be feeling pretty rotten. Sorry."

"Oh, it's all right."

"Sleep well, Elizabeth. I hope you'll be better to-morrow. Stay in bed till Sellyn comes."

We exchanged "good-nights," and he left.

I dropped off to sleep in an alien world for the first time in this adventure.

XV

I do not know what woke me up—a clock striking, I think. I came to with a start, thought of my home and to my surprise found myself in our sitting room. I was quite alone sitting in a chair near the fire.

I drew a deep breath and looked round, then I looked harder, for the room, my own room, was unfamiliar. It looked bigger and barer somehow. I discovered that the furniture had been re-arranged. How dare Elizabeth alter my house, though I could not deny that in some ways the room looked nicer. Where was Tom? He ought to be in bed.

I half decided to go and see, when he came in in his dressing gown. "Polly, what in Heaven's name are you doing? You must have finished all the sewing by now."

"Sewing?"

"Didn't you tell me you had things to finish off? Won't they keep till to-morrow? Do you realise it's two o'clock?"

I felt relieved. So she had not taken my place beside Tom. She had had that much decency at any rate. Well, I had resisted Gerald's fascination, but probably she was indifferent about that, which was why he was driven to be friendly with people like Leonora.

Tom was distinctly cross, he could not think why I had insisted on staying up. "And keeping that blazing fire going too, when you know what coals cost nowadays."

I then saw that the fire was heaped up, and was still more annoyed with Elizabeth; though I did reflect that she probably did not have to consider the price of fuel at Heringdon, and had perhaps not been extravagant on purpose.

Tom took off some of the coal, and raked out the fire, insisting that it was now bedtime.

"I suppose you were sitting admiring your arrangement of the room," he sniffed.

"Well, perhaps a change—sometimes—"

"I don't like having things upset when I'm used to them."

"Why didn't you say so then?" This was a feeler on my part.

"How the dickens could I say anything when you had it done before I got home? The only thing that pleased me about the whole business was your making that old fool Marshall help you to shift furniture; he was fairly dripping!"

I was bereft of speech. Mr Marshall moving furniture! After a moment's stupefaction I had to giggle at that.

"Perhaps it might stop him from coming here if you made him do it often."

"Well, I don't encourage him to come."

"H'm, then what got at you to promise that we'll go to the theatre with him next week and take Cousin Fanny? I thought you were potty."

I was staggered. Cousin Fanny! I could only murmur something about everyone having their potty moments.

I discovered later some more of Elizabeth's doings. She had wanted a bath before supper, and of course the water wouldn't heat up then, and, as I discovered from Gladys next morning, had ordered several things that we neither needed nor could afford, and I had a busy time counter-ordering and explaining to tradesmen that I had changed my mind.

The children were quite happy; they had been taken for walks and played with, and Bobby's cold was better. Evidently my visitor liked the children. I could not understand how she could be so kind to them and so unpleasant to me; perhaps she was jealous, as she had none of her own.

She had rather upset Tom also, commenting unfavourably on the way he brushed his hair and tied his tie. I found that out when he asked me if I was satisfied *now* about both these matters.

I hurriedly assured him that I liked him best the way he had been before, then he accused me of being capricious, looked at himself in the glass, and decided that I had been right in my criticism and that he owed it to his improved position in the firm to smarten up a little. He was still injured, however, about something "I" had said concerning his football club tie. She did seem to take the reins in my house. However, we replaced most of the furniture, though I maintained some of Elizabeth's alterations.

Tom kept on quoting her. He did not seem to have been altogether offended by her, but rather puzzled.

I wondered what had happened when she got back to Heringdon!

One of the most tiresome things she had done was arranging that hideous theatre party. I felt sure that Mr Marshall would drone the whole evening, Cousin Fanny complain, and Tom get fed up. I also felt sure that Elizabeth would *not* whisk me away on that occasion.

As I was supposed to have suggested the outing, it needed a good deal of diplomacy to discover when it was going to happen, and how I had got hold of Cousin Fanny. It was eventually revealed to me that she had dropped in when Mr Marshall was helping me to move furniture, and somehow or other I had induced the old boy to invite us all. We were to have high tea at my house, and Mr Marshall had arranged supper, after the play, at Lyons.

I wondered what Aunt Abigail thought.

Time passed on; I was not translated to Heringdon, and the day of the party arrived. I had a moment of vicious longing to get Elizabeth into my shoes when Fanny came round to ask what she should wear. She seemed disappointed when I did not advise her.

Needless to say Mr Marshall was punctual. He arrived while Tom, who had been kept late at the office, was still struggling with his clothes.

"This is indeed a festive occasion, little girl," said Mr Marshall, rubbing his hands. "I do not know what spell you worked on me to draw me from my quiet fireside. Many years ago I used to be a patron of the drama in the days of the great Irving, but since he left us for a higher sphere, the theatre has lost grace and lustre. You never saw Sir Henry, my child? No, no, you were born many years after he joined the immortals."

He then proceeded to tell me stories of plays that he had seen. I felt my jaws trembling in their efforts to avoid a yawn.

Mr Marshall's evening clothes were large and there seemed to be a great deal of his tie. Tom appeared at last, a little inclined to be cross, and Cousin Fanny arrived. She surprised me a good deal. Something had been done to her hair, her nose was powdered, she wore beads, and was smiling. An enquiry after Aunt Abigail removed the smile.

The old lady, it seemed, was feeling poorly and Fanny was terrified that she might be telephoned for before we could start for the theatre. A friend had been asked in to keep Aunt Abigail company for the evening; but if "spasms" were to come on, she still might summon Fanny.

During tea Mr Marshall continued his reminiscences; he impressed Fanny, who was thrilled, when he said that he had once known a man to speak to, who had understudied an actor who used to take Irving's parts on tour.

"I have often wondered what stage people are like," she said.

"Strange beings, dear lady," said Mr Marshall, "wandering through several lives, always living in two worlds. Bohemians, up to-day and down to-morrow, kings on the stage at one moment, beggars in the street the next, or beggars on the stage for an hour, and spoiled darlings in drawing rooms afterwards. I could tell you many things about them."

"How interesting," sighed Cousin Fanny. "I hear so little, mother's health obliges us to live so quietly."

"But young people must have a little pleasure, Miss Wardrop."

Cousin Fanny smirked and Tom's eyes began to twinkle. "Of course,

I know it's wrong to live entirely for pleasure, especially in times like these," said our relative, "but I feel that a little gaiety occasionally gives one something to think over afterwards."

"There is so much in life that is sad," said Mr Marshall, buttering a scone, "that one owes it to the world to smile when one can, through tears, if need be. A wounded heart need not be worn upon a sleeve." He sighed and took a large bite.

"Well, I hope the play won't wound our hearts," said Tom. "I like something laughable myself."

"What's it about?" enquired Fanny.

"I'm not quite sure." This from me.

"Why Polly, I took the seats on your warm recommendation," said Mr Marshall.

"I—I heard it was good." My misgivings were considerable; I mistrusted Elizabeth's choice.

When we went up to put on our coats and hats, Fanny asked me if Mr Marshall was not very intellectual. She wondered if his conversation would interest her mother. I suggested that she should ask him to tea, but she tittered and said she would never dare to invite a gentleman she knew so slightly.

When we went to catch the train, Mr Marshall walked on ahead with Fanny. It was a relief to be relieved from the droning of his voice for a time. Tom took my arm.

"They've 'clicked,' girlie! I wish he would drop in on Aunt Abigail instead of favouring us so much. It would be almost worth turning out on a cold night to achieve that; still I wish we were on our ownio, honeysuckle."

We had good seats in the dress circle and arrived in plenty of time. Mr Marshall bought a box of chocolates for Fanny and me.

The play was not very cheerful. From the programme I found out that it had been translated from the Rumanian. All the characters in it seemed unhappy. There was no real story. People came on and off the stage and talked at great length about their feelings. There was no proper hero or heroine, and the ones who made love were gloomy about it.

Some of the audience laughed at times, for no reason that I could see, but when a shock-headed tipsy man fell over a chair and Tom laughed, everybody round us said, "Ssh" loudly.

"The drama is changed since my time," said Mr Marshall in the interval. "I like a play with noble sentiment and fine acting, sound humour and gentle pathos."

"It doesn't make sense to me," said Tom. "Half the things these people do aren't sane."

Fanny remarked reproachfully that she was a little surprised at my taste.

I apologised, saying that the play had been recommended to me, but as I was a little vague as to the person who had given the advice, Tom suspected "Some of Syd's nonsense," and got decidedly grumpy in spite of my denials.

We stuck it out to the end, though Tom would have liked to leave, but I thought it would be rude to Mr Marshall, as he had bought the seats, and Cousin Fanny seemed to think it would be a pity to waste them as they had been paid for.

"It is saddening to an old man, to see what modern taste has come to," said Mr Marshall at supper, "but there were remarks in that piece which I do not think should be made before ladies, particularly unmarried ones."

"There was a great deal I did not understand," said Fanny.

"I don't mind a rude joke or so," said Tom. "A bit of spice livens a play up to my mind, but there was no go about this thing at all. The man made up to his bit, as if he was a doctor discussing a patient's symptoms. I'm glad of this Bass to take the taste of it out of my mouth."

We hurried over supper as Fanny was nervous about Aunt Abigail. So when we had taken her home, Mr Marshall came back with us as he was still hungry, and had some more beer and cold meat, which I had hoped to use up on the next day. He talked a good deal about the moral decline of the world, and the danger of foreign influence, and hoped that I would not allow it to affect me. I hastily reassured him, and told him and Tom that I must have made a mistake over the name of the play.

Eventually Mr Marshall left, hoping that we would meet again soon, and hoping that "that nice, modest girl, Miss Wardrop" had not been overtired or shocked.

Tom complained of a dud evening. He was only glad that "old Fanny and that blighter" had not enjoyed themselves either. "He won't spring a treat in a hurry again, I bet," he said. "I can't think how you got him to do it in the first place."

"Perhaps it had never occurred to him before."

"I hope it never does again. Lord, I'm tired. I say, old girl, I'm glad we don't live in Rumania, aren't you?" He kissed me.

"Perhaps it's not like that in reality," I said.

XVI

One of the results of the theatre party was that Aunt Abigail got ill. I do not know what the particular disease was, but she attributed it to neglecting to take some medicine or other that Fanny would have remembered to give her had she been there.

I called to enquire, taking Mr Marshall with me. Elizabeth's idea of moving him about, rather than letting him sit and boom, seemed a sound one. So that, when he arrived to call a few days after our theatre party, I bore him off at once to the Wardrops. He did not see Aunt Abigail, who was in bed, but Fanny, much to my relief, entertained him in the sitting room, while I visited the sick.

Aunt Abigail was very mournful and most spiteful about my having taken Fanny to see an improper play. That rumour had somehow gone round the family, and had made most of them laugh. Only Syd believed that I might have chosen the play for my own pleasure. He talked of it as a fine piece of work, and told me he had seen it from the gallery on the first night. The idea had entered his brain that I had highbrow leanings, and concealed them out of respect for my surroundings. I found it difficult to disabuse him. The way in which I had played at Christmas, and talked of music, made him sure that I had more knowledge than I pretended to have, and he treated me henceforth as one with whom he had a secret understanding, which was most inconvenient, and did not please Ethel or Tom.

Ethel's baby was born at the end of January, a dear little girl, and everybody was much excited. The christening was fixed for a month later, and I accepted an invitation to be Godmother with considerable trepidation, as I felt sure Elizabeth would try to butt in on such an occasion.

She gave no sign of life, however, and the only reminder I had of my other life was an encounter with the Rockleys.

It happened oddly enough.

There was an accident outside our house one afternoon; a little car skidded and bumped into a big one, which had a wheel damaged. I had run out to the gate to see whatever was to be seen, saw a lady and gentleman get out of the big car and, to my amazement, recognised them as the Rockleys.

Lady Rockley had been bumped against the window of the car, and had hurt her head a little. As her husband was attending to her, I went up to them and asked if they would care to come indoors and see what could be done to repair the damage.

They seemed grateful and came in, when Lord Rockley handed his wife over to my care, while he went back to help the chauffeur talk to a policeman who had bobbed up from somewhere.

Lady Rockley was not badly hurt, and I took her upstairs and applied Pond's Extract and got her a little brandy, thinking all the while of the last time I had met her. I thought what a shock I could give her, if I spoke of our last meeting.

When we came downstairs again, I found Lord Rockley talking to the children. I hoped, politely, that they had not bothered him. He replied that, on the contrary, he had been very well entertained, and added, "I must congratulate you on a wonderful talent for story-telling; I have been hearing marvels about goblins and ogres and magic stags."

"Oh, just a few things I make up to amuse the children," I said deprecatingly.

He continued: "I find also that we have a mutual affection for the same part of Scotland."

"Scotland!" I exclaimed, "I've never been there."

"Really, but surely Drinlaw Castle is in Scotland, and Kirrie Glen and the Burran Burn; I know all that part well."

"Are all those real places?" I cried, before I could stop myself.

His eyes lit up with interest. "Didn't you know?"

"I—I—thought they were just made-up names."

"How very interesting; you made up the names of a whole district, without ever having been there."

"Perhaps you read about it," said Lady Rockley, in a matter-of-fact tone.

"Perhaps I did and have forgotten; I expect that's it," said I, relieved at the way out.

"But have you forgotten?" he enquired. "It is certainly very remarkable. Do tell me if …"

His wife interrupted him. "Arthur, darling, really you mustn't cross-examine people." She turned smiling to me. "You must forgive my husband, he has an overwhelming interest in curious psychical happenings, and is always on the look-out for them."

I nodded. "Everyone knows of Lord Rockley's researches," I said politely.

That seemed to surprise them a good deal, as did the fact that I had recognised them, but I bungled through some sort of explanation of how they had been pointed out to me somewhere or other.

Soon after that the taxi for which they had sent, arrived. They said "good-bye" very politely and thanked me for my kindness, and I had a very nice letter and some flowers from Lady Rockley next day. I wondered what Lord Rockley would think if he knew my story; there were some parts of it that would be a little difficult to tell.

Tom teased me about my friendship with the grandees, and asked if I had arranged for the accident to take place in front of my door, so as to give me a chance of getting into society; but I think he was sorry that he had missed them himself.

XVII

I thought that I had heard the last of Lord Rockley, but about a week later I received a letter from him. It was very short and quite kind, merely stating that, as a psychic investigator, he would be glad to hear of any experience of mine, which would be interesting.

Tom saw the letter, which arrived at breakfast time, noticed the coronet on the envelope, and enquired of me, whether I had been corresponding with the King, as "crowned" letters came for me.

"It's not a crown, only a coronet," I said.

"Indeed! Are you starting a correspondence with the noble lord whom chance brought here the other day? I'll have something to say about that."

"Why, Tom? He only writes about a book that we happened to mention."

"The dickens he does! Well, I'm not going to have strange men writing to my wife. That's flat."

"Tom, don't you trust me?" I queried, reproachfully.

"I don't trust *him*; all these swells have soft-soaping ways. If he bothers you I shall give him a pretty clear hint to mind his own business."

"Tom, Lord Rockley is not at all that sort of man; he's got a very nice wife and he's very fond of her."

"H'm. I've got a very nice wife I'm very fond of, but I expect I should hear something from you if I wrote letters to another woman."

It took me quite a long time to smooth Tom down and, though he became more amiable, I could see that he was still suspicious of Lord

Rockley. It crossed my mind then, that perhaps there was something a little barbarous about Tom's attitude. Could neither a husband nor a wife have a personal friend? There might be men I should like to talk to who would bore Tom, and there might be women with whom Tom would like to talk, who might find that I had nothing in common with them. Enjoying the company of a member of the opposite sex did not always entail an intrigue. I was not thinking of Lord Rockley in particular, only of people in general. I had never thought in this way before, because all our friends, Tom's and mine, were mutual.

Naturally, I should have hated it if he had friends like Leonora—but still— Suddenly I wondered how much of this was Elizabeth's influence. Certainly it was owing to her that I had secrets from Tom, which I did not like doing. Was all this going to make us unhappy together?

Life is very complicated when you cannot explain things to the people you love best. I did not answer Lord Rockley's letter, because I could not decide what to say, nor did I want to hide his possible reply from Tom.

Ethel's baby girl was christened early in February without mishap. I had had a very short translation to Heringdon the day before the christening, or rather, the night. It happened like this.

I woke up in the middle of the night, which is a thing I hardly ever do, the cause of this being a lump in the mattress that bothered me. I tried to manoeuvre myself off it, carefully, so as not to wake Tom, and my thoughts flew to the lovely bed at Heringdon, where, in a flash, I found myself.

I was alone in it, and very uncomfortable, with a sore throat and a buzzing in my ears. I turned on the light and tried to call out, but could not. I was furious and afraid; was Elizabeth very ill, or did she mean me to die instead of her? I felt too wobbly to get up, but I suppose I must have made a noise of some kind, because a nurse appeared from somewhere, and tried to make me comfortable. Flinging caution to the winds, I asked her how ill she thought me, and she told me that I was no worse than yesterday, and that influenza must run its course; she seemed rather surprised at my agitation.

I gave that nurse a good deal of trouble, as I was sick with rage at the thought of Elizabeth in bed with Tom, but I very soon escaped and found myself home again.

I "came to" sitting in a chair in the children's room, frozen to the marrow. Both kids were asleep, as I could see by the gleam of their night-light which was peacefully burning away in the corner as usual.

I flew to Tom as soon as I had assured myself that the children were safe, and found him awake and worried. It came out in conversation that I had woken him up by "squeaking" as he called it, and he thought I was having a nightmare. He had tried to comfort me, but I had turned on the light and mumbled something about being nervous about the kids, and run out of the room.

I could not understand Elizabeth. Surely she must have expected to find Tom in bed in the middle of the night? Had her conscience pricked her, or was it revenge? Should I ever know?

I did not sleep any more that night, and had a cold next day, which, however, did not turn into influenza, as for a time I had feared it might.

I went to the christening with a red nose. Ethel and Syd had quite a little party. His parents, of course, and Tom and me, and Aunt Abigail, Cousin Fanny, Mabel and George, and Mr Marshall, besides a few more friends. Aunt Abigail said at tea how sad christenings always made her, when she thought of the trials and temptations waiting for the poor little child on its way through life, but Fanny, who seemed to have taken to disagreeing with her lately, said quite sharply that there were happy times as well as unhappy, waiting for us all.

"I agree with you, Miss Wardrop," said Mr Marshall. "Who would refuse the glorious adventure of life, because there may be stones on the road over which we travel; and the hearth is a lonely one, near which the pattering of little feet is never heard." He sighed heavily.

"The pattering comes a bit expensive sometimes," grinned George, "when the little dears patter through their shoes and need new ones; you'll find that out, Syd, my boy."

"Some people don't like children," said I, thinking of Leonora.

"They must be hard-hearted," cooed Cousin Fanny, which surprised me a little, because I had always thought children bored her.

"It is a pleasure to an old man, watching the generations succeed one another," boomed Mr Marshall. "Little copies of well-beloved folks treading in their parents' footsteps."

"And in their own obstinate ways sometimes," sniffed Aunt Abigail. "Growing up, forgetting all that their parents have tried to teach them, as you'd know if you'd ever had any, Mr Marshall."

"I am sure that Mr Marshall would have been a very kind father," said Cousin Fanny, looking down.

"Well, it's not too late for him to try," sniggered George. "Find a wife, Marshall, and when you've got half a dozen kids …"

"I live in my memories," said Mr Marshall gravely.

"Very comfortably, too," whispered Tom to me.

Sydney's father now changed the subject by suggesting that we should drink the baby's health, and the sherry and port were opened, and things became more cheerful. Naturally, Mr Marshall made a speech—a good long one with a great deal in it about bringing up children in the good old English way, and avoiding all pernicious foreign influences. He glanced at me when he arrived at this point, though I saw Sydney getting a little restive.

Cousin Fanny complimented him when he had finished, and asked him why he had never gone in for politics.

Mr Marshall replied that his little business had filled his early years with toil, and that, now he had retired, the hurly-burly of the modern world had passed him by.

"I am not ambitious," he said. "I love the simple homely things, my hearth, my friends, my faithful dog, my books and thoughts."

"You are a great thinker, Mr Marshall," Cousin Fanny said respectfully.

"And a greater talker," whispered Tom.

On the way home Tom and I laughed over the idea of Mr Marshall with a wife and family.

"He wouldn't keep the wife long, she'd end in an asylum," said Tom. "How I understand that woman's jilting him years ago."

"Cousin Fanny seems to like him," I said.

"Aunt Abigail doesn't," retorted Tom, "which is a pity, as he might go and boom at them instead of at us."

"He's been there quite often, I believe," I said.

A few days later I saw in the papers that the marriage of Mr Anthony Launde and the Hon. Phyllis Brent would take place next day.

I felt that I must go and see that wedding, for which I could not help feeling responsible; so made an excuse and went up to Town.

I arrived outside the church while the wedding was still going on. With the help of a little gentle pushing, I got myself a place in the crowd, from where I could see everybody come out of church. It was not such a very big wedding and there was not a very dense crowd.

Phyllis emerged at last, with her arm through Toby's. I felt glad that it *was* Toby. They were both beaming, and from my heart I sent them every sort of good wish. Then I moved slowly, a little away along the pavement, watching the guests come out of church and get into their cars. Suddenly, quite close to me I saw Gerald. There was no mistaking him; he was walking with a pretty, smartly dressed, red-haired woman. I thought how I could make him jump by going up to him and addressing him by his Christian name.

He paused by the kerb, still talking to the red-haired lady, and was joined by two more ladies. One was Mrs Forrester, but the other …

The other … at first I had not noticed her particularly, but as she was speaking to Gerald, her face turned in my direction and I knew her— knew her features that I had seen in looking-glasses, the long lashes I had blinked through …

I stood still, trembling all over, unable to move. She turned still more in my direction, and our eyes met. It could not have been for more than a few seconds that we stared at each other, yet it seemed a long time.

I knew my eyes were goggling, my mouth open—her expression was one of blank surprise, then it changed, unmistakably changed to a look of dislike, and ... there could be no doubt about it ... fear.

I think it was Mrs Forrester touching her on the arm, which made her pull herself together; in a flash her face was calm and she turned away.

The big car that I remembered drew up beside the pavement and they all four got into it.

I felt as if I was going to faint—closed my eyes, and opened them ... in that car.

XVIII

I found myself sitting between the strange woman and Mrs Forrester. Gerald was on the small seat facing us.

Mrs Forrester asked me if I was feeling faint; no doubt she had seen me, or rather Elizabeth, closing my eyes. As quickly as I could manage to speak, I said that the church had been rather hot, but that I was all right now.

I did not particularly mind this switch, as it pleased me to go to Phyllis' wedding. The only thing that bothered me was that I had arranged to meet Millie Rayne and her sister at a Picture House at five, and I did not believe that Elizabeth would keep my appointment. How could she? I was surprised that she had allowed me to attend this gathering, which I should enjoy.

There had been no mistaking her look of dislike when she had caught sight of me, but what had really surprised me was her look of fear.

My fellow travellers discussed the ceremony, and Gerald told the strange lady, whose name I eventually discovered was Mrs Farnborough, that Phyllis and Toby had got engaged at Heringdon.

"What fun. Did you make the match, Lady Elizabeth?" she asked.

"I think it made itself," I replied.

"I'm not sure that you didn't give it a shove, though," said Gerald.

"Oh, I'm all for people being happy," said I, brightly.

"Well, I hope your wishes will be realised, but I should think there's every chance of those two finding themselves in the workhouse in a couple of years' time."

"Oh, let's hope not," laughed Mrs Forrester.

They talked on about Phyllis and Toby, their prospects and relations, and then we stopped at a house with an awning, and Mrs Farnborough thanked us for the lift. There seemed to be a good many people in the house. Gerald said things about a "damned squash."

We got up the stairs and a large butler bent down to ask my name. "Lady Forrester and Major Forrester," I said.

The names were boomed out, and I soon found myself being embraced by Phyllis. I do not remember what I said to her, but I know that there were tears in my eyes. Brides always make me feel weepy. Toby shook my hand very hard, and then laughed at something Gerald said to him.

We moved on, and I wiped my eyes on a handkerchief that I took out of Elizabeth's bag, a wretched little wisp of a thing, I thought it. I like one on which one can really blow one's nose properly.

"Got something in your eye?" enquired Gerald.

"Nothing much ... I'm glad to see Phyllis happy, that's all."

He had no time to say anything before we found ourselves shaking hands with two people, who, I imagined, must be the bride's parents. We said some politeness or other and oozed onward in a stream of people.

I could not greet by name all the strangers who now talked to me, though I felt sure that I had seen some of their faces in the papers. Gerald had drifted away somewhere and I felt a little lost, though interested.

A tall man, with grey hair and moustache, tapped me on the shoulder, saying:

"You're a nice daughter, cutting your own father."

"Oh!" I jumped out of my skin. This was the man whose letter I had read. "I ... I didn't see you."

"You must have gone suddenly blind, then, for you've been staring at me for the last five minutes."

"I'm sorry."

"I saw Gerald just now talking to a devilish pretty woman with red hair."

"Mrs Farnborough?"

"Is that her name? Is she his latest?"

"I ... I really don't know." I was shocked by his asking me that, though I could see he was laughing.

"Hullo, darling," gurgled a musical voice in my ear, and I turned to face Leonora.

"How do you do?" I said. "It seems a long time since we met."

"Is that a compliment darling, or have you forgotten that we both lunched with Clarice yesterday?"

"I ... I had forgotten, I'm afraid."

"What do you think of that, Lord Wantage?" laughed Leonora.

"I should not have thought you could have been easily overlooked," said the old gentleman.

"Talking of which, where's Gerald?" said Leonora. "I haven't seen him for ages."

"He's here somewhere." I looked round vaguely. "With Mrs Farnborough, I believe."

"Oh, Carroty Kate, such a bore the woman is."

"I don't think Gerald finds her so," I said.

Leonora laughed, but her eyes did not look pleased. "He soon will, unless he goes deaf."

At that moment Lord Rockley came up and talked to us. He told us, in answer to a question of Lord Wantage's, that his wife had not come to the wedding as she was feeling rather seedy.

"Not the result of the motor accident, I hope?" I said.

"No—the remains of 'flu, but how did you hear we had a motor smash? It was nothing really. Moira had a slight bump that's all."

"Somebody must have told me," I said quickly.

Lord Wantage looked at me rather hard. "Not second sight?" he queried.

"Second sight? Have you second sight?" said Rockley interestedly.

"But how too thrilling, darling! Have you kept it a secret like your bridge playing?" said Leonora.

"Oh, no," I said, embarrassed. "I have no strange powers at all."

"I am very glad," said Lord Wantage. "With all respect to you, Rockley, I think such things are better left alone."

"But what made you suspect Elizabeth of second sight?" said Leonora.

"Well, she wrote to me some time ago, asking if any of our family had ever been hypnotic subjects, or received telepathic messages."

"What made you wonder that, Lady Elizabeth?" said Rockley. "Have you had any strange experiences?"

"Oh, no," I said. "Not really—"

Then much to my relief, a little man wearing an eye-glass bustled up to our group.

"Well, 'Lady Forrester,'" he giggled. "What a mutt that hireling must be."

"What do you mean?" I gasped.

"I came upstairs just behind you and heard him announce you and Gerald as, 'Lady and Major Forrester.'"

"Well, what's wrong in that … he said what I told him to say," I remarked, thinking the little man silly.

"Darling, you're wool-gathering," said Leonora. "First you forget your name, then you forget you saw me yesterday."

"And then your father," put in Lord Wantage.

"Oh, not really, Dad," I said hastily.

They laughed at that as if I had made a joke, and the little man said that he thought the atmosphere of the room was enough to make anyone forget anything.

Then he enquired if Gerald was there, and being answered in the affirmative, said to Leonora:

"I suppose I needn't ask if Giles is present?"

"No, you needn't," she laughed. "This sort of thing is hardly Giles' cocktail."

Soon after that the little man left us, and Leonora remarked:

"I do think being a gossip writer is a lousy job for a man, don't you?"

"Oh, is he a gossip writer?" I stared after him with curiosity.

"Elizabeth, you're not going to tell me that you've forgotten that about Tips Farlow. Have you lost your memory or something?"

"Of course not," I snapped. "I was thinking of something else for the moment."

"Do come and look at the presents, Lady Elizabeth," Lord Rockley's voice broke in at this juncture.

I went with him gladly, only saying: "See you later, Dad," to Elizabeth's father.

"If you call me 'Dad' again, I shall address you as 'Betsy,'" said the old gentleman as we went off.

I wondered what I ought to have called him. 'Dad' seemed so natural somehow, but once again something natural to me seemed wrong for Elizabeth.

Lord Rockley asked me if I would like to come into another room outside and get some air. I asked him if he thought I looked ill.

"Oh, no," he answered me, "but I thought when I saw you first that you looked a little bewildered somehow, and wondered if you were feeling faint or anything." He was looking at me intently, as he had done that day at Heringdon.

I decided not to risk too much conversation with him, so said:

"I wouldn't miss the presents for anything."

There was a crowd in the room where the presents were, but I managed to see most of them. I thought that the couple had been given a tremendous lot of things. Lord Rockley asked what 'I and Forrester' had given.

"Something we thought they'd like," I parried.

"Is it a secret?"

"If it is, try and find it out," I smiled.

Just then somebody stopped him to talk, and I moved unobtrusively on. Knowing him in two lives was most confusing. I was afraid of giving myself away. I remembered that I had not answered his letter.

Somebody laid a hand on my arm—Mrs Forrester. "To him that hath shall be given," she murmured. "Think of June Fordyce's wedding last week, but then she was marrying a millionaire, so naturally her presents were magnificent."

"Don't you think these are nice?" I asked.

"Oh well,"—she shrugged her shoulders.

At that moment somebody told us that the bride was cutting the cake, and we went downstairs to see her do it. I met and spoke to Lady Pottlesham, but as I let her do most of the talking I avoided any blunders.

People were eating, and drinking champagne, but nobody made a speech or anything like that. Somebody gave me a glass, and I sipped the fizzy contents to the health and happiness of Phyllis and Toby.

Later on a girl came in and told me that Phyllis had changed. She seemed surprised that I had not been up to see her already. "Phyllis has been asking for you," she said.

I remembered that the engagement had taken place at Heringdon, as I followed my leader upstairs to a bedroom, full of Phyllis, women and girls.

"What happened to you, Eliza?" cried Phyllis.

"I didn't know you'd be ready so soon," said I, as the best explanation I could think of for my tardiness.

"Absent-minded creature, who was there when we looked out the train?"

"Are you happy, Phyllis?" I asked softly.

"Perhaps I shall be when Toby and I have got through the *voyage de noces* and settled down in our slum."

"Slum!" I exclaimed. "You're never going to live in a slum?"

"Darling, don't be funny at me on my wedding day."

"I'm not feeling in the least funny. I wish you every possible sort of happiness, you know that, Phyllis; and if you and Toby care for each other, as I think you do, you'll get it."

She was quite close to me, and suddenly said:

"Eliza, I do believe you've got tears in your eyes. You are a sentimental being, then, under that icy exterior."

"Oh, my dear," I said, and we found ourselves embracing each other warmly.

"God bless you and Toby too," I whispered in her ear.

Somebody—her mother, I think, came and said things about hurrying, and then everything was bustle. Voices called out that Toby was waiting, and I was swept out of the room in Phyllis' wake.

In a very short time, bride and bridegroom had left, passing through showers of rice and paper rose-leaves into a car, and away.

The guests began to go away.

I wondered where Gerald was, and Mrs Forrester. I found the latter in the company of Lord Rockley.

"Ah, there you are, Elizabeth. We ought to go. I have just been talking spooks to Lord Rockley."

"Oh."

"I told him about the times when your dogs behaved so queerly."

"Perhaps something frightened them," I said casually.

"Certainly," said Mrs Forrester, "but what?"

"It was as if something stood near you that they did not like."

"Very curious." His eyes were on my face.

"Have they behaved like that again?"

"No, we are quite friends now," I said.

"Are we going to stay here all day, now that the execution's over?" Gerald's voice broke in on our conversation.

"We were just waiting to say good-bye to Mary Windlesham," said Mrs Forrester.

We said good-bye to Lord Rockley, who told me that we were to meet at dinner that night; then we went through more farewells with the Windleshams and finally departed in the car.

We dropped Mrs Forrester at a house where she was going to play bridge, and then Gerald asked me if I would shoot him out at his club.

I felt shy at being alone with him again after our last meeting. But he certainly did not seem to be in an affectionate mood to-day as far as I was concerned.

"Aren't you coming with me?" I asked.

"I'll be home in time to dress."

"That isn't very sociable," I said. "I've hardly seen you all day. You were so busy talking to that Mrs Farnborough, weren't you?"

"She seems rather good value. You might ask her to dinner some time. Why not when we're up next week?"

"I think she's rather too attractive."

"What do you mean? Are we condemned to invite only gargoyles?"

"Won't Leonora be jealous. She was complaining to-day that she never saw you now."

He only grunted in reply.

An imp of mischief seemed to be prompting me.

"Gerald, didn't that wedding make you think of ours?" I enquired softly.

"I suppose all weddings are more or less alike," he said drily. "The same unpleasant and unnecessary orgy."

"How can you?" said I, shocked. "Why surely, one's wedding day is the most wonderful day of one's life to look back on and remember."

"It's funny you should say that," said Gerald, looking at me rather hard.

"Why?" I enquired, prompted by curiosity. "Do you think that I regret my marriage?"

"That's a question you can answer better than I can, my dear, though it is true that sometimes lately you've seemed a little undecided about it."

Before I could guess what should be my right answer, the car stopped at

Gerald's club. He got out quickly, seeming relieved that our conversation was ended for the moment, and asked me if I wanted to go home.

"What, all the way to Heringdon?" I cried, startled.

"Heringdon? What are you talking about?"

"I ... I always think of Heringdon as home."

He frowned impatiently. "Shall I tell him to go to Branksome Square or not?"

"I may as well go there as anywhere."

He said something to the chauffeur, who shut the door, got into the front of the car and drove on.

So the Forresters had a house in London. It seemed to bring them uncomfortably nearer; yet I felt interested, and wanted to see what it was like.

I also wanted to find out exactly what the relations were between Gerald and his wife. Did he like her, or did he not? He was bitter to her, but I remembered that night at Heringdon, and that perhaps—I blushed when I thought of it. Yet he admired other women, and seemed to expect her not to mind. Would he mind if she flirted with other men?

The car stopped at a house and the chauffeur got out and rang the bell. The door was opened by a footman. He said to me that somebody was waiting to see me in the morning-room.

"Who is it?"

"I don't know, my lady. She refused to give any name, but said she would wait for your ladyship."

"Well ... I suppose I had better see her."

He ushered me into a room and closed the door behind me.

A woman got up from a sofa. My knees grew weak and I sank into the chair behind me, for there, standing facing me, was myself.

XIX

Of all the weird things that had happened to me during this adventure, I think that this was the weirdest.

Seeing Elizabeth's face in my mirror was nothing in comparison to it.

I also discovered that, however well one knows one's aspect in looking glasses, the reality is quite different. My figure was more solid than I had imagined it to be. On my borrowed face the present tenant had put an expression that I felt sure I could never have managed.

There was silence for one tense moment, then she spoke through my trembling lips.

"I thought you might come here."

The sound of my own voice controlled by an alien personality, proceeding from my mouth, gave me a shock. I turned giddy.

It was as though I was caught in a whirlpool. I emerged from the topsy-turviness to find myself safely back in my own skin, standing opposite Elizabeth.

I gasped and clutched the nearest chair.

She was pale, and her eyes were still closed. There was no doubt of her being beautiful. She did not look as cruel as I had expected her to do.

A moment later she opened her eyes and looked at me in a half-angry, half-frightened way.

"Do you mind if I sit down?" was all that I could manage to say.

She nodded and seemed to be trying to pull herself together. Then she spoke:

"Why have you done this to me, Mrs Wilkinson?" Her voice was low and trembled.

I was wordless, staring at her. She went on:

"Why do you use this dreadful power of yours on me? I have never hurt you."

I recovered my voice with an effort.

"My power, Lady Forrester? Mine?"

My astonishment was so obvious that it convinced her of its truth. She grew paler still.

"Mrs Wilkinson, do you mean to tell me that you are not responsible for this extraordinary thing that has happened to us both?"

"Responsible?" I cried. "Why, I've been putting it all down to you, and wondering how you could have the heart to play me all those pranks."

"Then this happens to us without our own volition, for no discoverable rhyme or reason?"

"Seems like it."

"Why to us two out of all the people in the world?"

"I don't know. The question is, what are we to do about it?"

There was another silence. Then she asked:

"Have you told anybody about it?"

"No, have you?"

"No, how could one?" She made a helpless sort of gesture.

"That's what I feel too."

Another pause.

"What started it?" she said. "What sort of an affinity is there between us?"

"I don't know. I—I—had never even heard of you before this happened."

"Nor I of you."

"What had we in common?"

I spoke: "The first transformation was in last September when I found myself in a room with Mrs Forrester about ten o'clock at night."

"With my mother-in-law ... yes ... I remember. I found myself in your house alone, went to explore and came across your children asleep. I thought I had been dreaming."

"So did I, but the dogs spotted something."

"I know, my mother-in-law thought they had seen a ghost."

"They knew that you were not you," I said, and went on, "but the children knew nothing; they never thought that there was anything different any of the times." I could not help chuckling as I added: "You gave me some trouble trying to keep up with your stories."

She flushed a little.

"The children are rather sweet, somehow it seemed only natural to play with them."

"Evidently," I said, rather drily. Then curiosity awoke in me. "You don't dislike children then?"

"No—why should I?"

I felt confused. "Oh—just—I don't know—"

"Because I have none?"

"Oh, well, those things are luck, of course," I said hastily.

Her face expression saddened. She spoke as if half to herself. "Luck … yes … no doubt. I was going to have one once, but … there was an accident … and it was just about that time that …" She stopped short, and her expression changed, as she said: "But what are we doing—two complete strangers—sitting talking like this? Are we mad or dreaming, or what?"

"Neither," I retorted. "It's only too real; we know that by the effect these … er … switch-overs have on our surroundings."

"Oh, yes," a faint smile came over her face. "Do tell me—are Cousin Fanny and Mr Marshall engaged yet?"

"Cousin Fanny, Mr Marshall?" I was amazed. "But they aren't the marrying kind."

"What makes you think that? Mr Marshall is lonely, poor Cousin Fanny is victimised by that tyrannical old mother of hers. She's bursting to have all sorts of fun, but she daren't."

"She wouldn't have much fun with Mr Marshall."

"Oh, I don't know; she probably admires him tremendously, and he'd love having her for an audience. What a wonderful couple they'd make. You really must encourage them Mrs Wilkinson."

"I—really, I don't see how."

"Nonsense. Throw them together and it will happen."

"I don't know if that would work. The play you chose for me to take them to wasn't a great success."

She laughed. "Wasn't it? It was a very good play. Still, I'm sure their mutual disapproval of it created a bond of sympathy between them. I shouldn't worry; besides, you have a talent for match-making, haven't you? What about Phyllis Brent and Toby Launde? You married them, didn't you?"

"I think they always wanted to marry each other, only they were afraid of being thought imprudent," I said, stiffly.

"I think they were imprudent," said she, "but most marriages are, I suppose."

"Oh … are you cynical too?"

"Too?"

"Like Gerald, I—I mean, Major Forrester." I went hot all over.

"Gerald—oh yes." The expression seemed somehow to fade out of her face. "You seem to have talked fairly freely to Gerald, Mrs Wilkinson."

"Oh, well—the position was a little difficult. I don't think I did anything very bad. I didn't ask to be in your place, you know."

"Of course not. It was an unprecedented situation." Then just the very faintest shadow of a smile showed on her lips. "I think Gerald found himself a little bewildered," she said.

"Nothing to what Tom did," I rejoined, hotly. "You thoroughly upset him, Lady Forrester. Why did you do it?"

"Upset Tom—your husband? Wasn't I nice to him? But I thought him a dear. He seemed so kind and reliable."

"You turned his house upside down."

"I only made some experiments; you see I did not know that it wasn't your fault my being there at all. Did I do anything else wrong?"

"Well, what about the flirtations?"

"Flirtations?" She sat up straight.

"What about Mr Sparlow on Christmas night? I had quite a business putting him in his place afterwards."

"Mr Sparlow—oh, the young man who danced quite well; I don't remember any particularly intimate conversation with him."

"You called him 'Jack' and asked him to dance."

"I took him for a family friend and called him 'Jack' as your husband did. As for the dancing, I thought the party needed enlivening a little, so I started them off."

"But Syd?"

"Syd?—Oh, your brother-in-law. But he's charming, and very intelligent."

"But—" I checked myself, remembering the whole situation, and added in a calmer tone. "Well, of course you had no reason to feel friendly towards me. I was furious with you for taking me away from home on Christmas Day."

"You certainly made some trouble for me on my return," she said, drily.

"But all this isn't getting us any nearer the solution of our problem; are we going to play 'Puss in the Corner' with each other for ever?"

"I wish I knew. Perhaps it might help if we could find out how it all started—that first time we changed. What were you doing that evening?"

I thought hard.

"Waiting for Tom to come home from a dinner. I had been sewing, then I took up a magazine; there was a picture of a car in it, very much like your car—"

"My car—how did you know it was mine?"

"I've seen it since."

"Since—yes, but when—"

"Well, I had seen it a week before, when it got stuck where they were repairing Barling Road."

"How very extraordinary."

"Why?"

"Never mind, go on, tell me about the time when you saw the car."

I thought, and remembered that September evening and how tired I was. I told her about it; how I had watched the motor go by and seen a woman's figure in it, and had wished to change places with whomever it might be.

Her eyes seemed to get larger as she listened to me.

"That's extraordinary," she said, in a low voice. "I remember that evening perfectly, and the car stopping just at that spot. I was worried about—several things, and I saw a gleam of light from the open door of a little house, and the house looked so friendly somehow. I saw a woman leaning on the garden gate, and thought that … that she was probably waiting for someone … someone who would be pleased to see her, and that when, whoever it was, arrived, they would go into the house, shut the door and sit down comfortably together—with their family perhaps— and I wished to change places with that woman …" She stopped. I drew a deep breath.

"So that's what we had in common; we both wanted to escape, and we thought about it at the same moment."

"But that's all that happened at the time. It doesn't account for—no, wait a moment. On that evening a week later, I was thinking of the house in Barling Road. I don't remember what started the train of thought, but I seemed to see a mental picture of the house, with the light from the door, the woman leaning over the gate—then I got giddy, and …"

"At about ten o'clock!" I exclaimed.

"Yes."

"We were both thinking of each other at the same moment, and we *did* change places and didn't know it at first—at least I didn't, did you?"

"No, I thought I had dreamed the home with the children in it, just as I had fancied it might be."

And the next time, when I found myself on the drive at Heringdon, and those ladies came to tea—"

She nodded.

"I remember. I was alarmed then because I remembered nothing about their visit when Mrs Forrester referred to it. I thought I was suffering from some form of somnambulism, and had dreamed my afternoon in Barling Road with your children and Ethel."

"Did you ever think you were going mad? I did."

"No, I think I pretty nearly guessed the truth after that time when you took my place, while we had people staying for a shoot. Yet it all seemed so incredible that I did not fully believe it until after Christmas. Then I felt sure that I was under your influence. I wondered what to do. I thought of approaching you, but dared not write."

"Just like me."

"I even went to Barling Road one evening, but turned back when I saw your husband going into the house."

"Did you drive up to our door?" I queried curiously.

"No, just along the road, in a taxi."

"If all this depends on our thoughts coinciding," said I, slowly, "we ought to be able to manage to stop it."

"But we are thinking of each other now, we must be, and yet no change is taking place; this force—whatever it is, must be potent only under certain conditions."

"And we don't know what they are, either of us," I exclaimed.

"And it is hardly a case about which one could consult a doctor," she said.

"Any doctor would think us mad."

"Yes, we both seem to have acquired a reputation for eccentric behaviour," she said, drily. "Still, no one is likely to suspect the truth."

"The only man who might is Lord Rockley," I said. "I'm sure he thinks you have a dual personality."

"Lord Rockley—oh yes, of course he was there when—I have noticed his intense interest in me."

"I saw him at the wedding reception to-day," I said.

"Good Lord, yes, Phyllis' wedding! You were there, of course. Later on you must tell me about the people you talked to, and save me from making too many pies—but first—"

Before she could say any more, the door opened and Gerald came in.

XX

He strolled in quite slowly, seeming, I thought, slightly surprised when he saw me. I felt extremely queer. It was so funny to be greeting him like this after the talks we had had. I felt shy.

Elizabeth showed no enthusiasm at his return. I reflected that Tom would not be pleased if I looked at him as though he were just anybody, when he came home.

"Oh, Gerald, I don't think you've met Mrs Wilkinson."

I got up and held out my hand.

He shook it and said, "How do you do?" politely.

It was all I could do not to laugh, though I felt embarrassment as well. He said something about the evening being cold.

"I ought to be going, Lady Forrester," I remarked.

"Oh, are you in any particular hurry?"

"It's getting late. Mr Wilkinson will be expecting me."

"And don't forget we are dining early for the play, my dear," said Gerald.

"I won't keep you," I said, "so it really must be 'good-bye' now."

She rang the bell. I shook hands with them again.

"We must meet again, Mrs Wilkinson. I'll write to you."

"Yes, you know my address." I giggled.

A footman came in, and subsequently let me out of the house. I departed, thinking that I had just taken part in what must have been the most extraordinary interview in the world's history.

I was late getting home, and found Tom upset. Millie Rayne and her sister had waited for me for ages at the picture house, nearly missed the beginning of the big film and, on their return, Millie had telephoned to ask why I had never turned up. I told Tom that my shopping had taken much longer than I had expected, that I had forgotten the time, felt sure that my friends would not wait for me, that I might never find them in the cinema and had gone to another picture by myself.

Above all things in the world I hate deceiving Tom; I suppose this must have been evident in my manner, because he looked at me suspiciously and accepted my explanation with a grunt.

He asked what the picture was, but, having had time to prepare my story on the way home, I gave him the name of one, quite naturally. The matter might have passed off all right, but next day Ethel dropped in to tea, and asked what I had been doing in Hyde Park the day before.

She said that Ellie Dunton had seen me there "looking ever so worried" and that I had paid no attention to Ellie at all. I said that Ellie must have made a mistake, and taken somebody else for me and wished that I had asked Elizabeth where she had taken my body after the wedding, before she went back to her own house.

After Ethel left, Tom and I had a row. He accused me of being secretive, and said that he had felt sure for some time that there was something I had been keeping from him. I asked him if I was the sort of person who habitually told untruths, and enquired what he suspected. He harped again on the subject of Lord Rockley, and the letter from that gentleman, which I had never shown him, and said that he was jolly well not going to be fooled as Percy Springer was by Nettie.

I was furious then, and asked him how he dared mention me in the same breath with a woman like that, who had actually been divorced. We got angrier and angrier, and then I cried so much that I gave myself a headache, after which Tom began to think that perhaps he had gone too far, and comforted me, so we made it up and he swore that he trusted me, but said it would kill him if he ever discovered that I had deceived him.

I got up early next morning and was down when the postman came, because I had a feeling that there might be a letter from Lady Elizabeth which would be just as unexplainable as Lord Rockley's.

I was right; there was a letter, on nice paper, directed in a strange handwriting, and I hid it until Tom was safely on his way to the office.

Elizabeth asked me to come and see her soon, at her London house. She gave me the choice of several days and times, enquiring which would be most convenient.

That took some thinking out. Tom was at the office all day, but he generally wanted to hear what I had been doing when he came home; also, leaving the house for any length of time meant fixing up the children somehow, because the maids were not as a rule anxious to be left in charge of them; besides, what with one thing and another, I am usually pretty busy all day. Somebody generally knew where I was going, or what I was doing.

It occurred to me then, that I really had no private life at all. I had never objected before, and I suppose that I should not have done so now, had I not had something to hide.

I thought of Elizabeth. Gerald would never ask what she had been doing, and she could go to a picture gallery or a concert and nobody would think it at all queer, whereas if I should feel inclined to do something quite ordinary like that, by myself, everybody in my neighbourhood would wonder why. Even letters were a little difficult. Tom did not want to read my letters, but he always asked from whom they came.

In the early days of our marriage I still managed to correspond with school friends, but somehow, with a household and children to look after, there had gradually seemed to be less and less time just for writing talky-talky letters, and my post had got smaller and smaller.

Still, I thought I could manage about letters. I was pondering on ways and means of getting a day off in order to visit Elizabeth, when it became an impossibility, owing to Bobby spraining his ankle.

The injury was not a serious one, but the child had to be kept quiet for a day or so, which meant that I would be obliged to stay with him most of the time. I wrote, therefore, to Elizabeth, and told her that I could not come this week at any rate. She replied, in a very nice letter, sympathising about Bobby's mishap, and telling me that she was going to Heringdon at the end of the week, but could run up some day, if I would let her know in good time.

She also sent some toys for Bobby. Luckily they arrived when Tom was out, and I hid some of them, or he would have wondered how I could have afforded to buy such lovely ones. I let Bobby have some of them, which delighted him more than Tom, who was not so pleased when he found his son in possession of better playthings than some he had brought home for him.

I wrote again to Elizabeth and asked her not to send anything to any of us, as presents were too difficult to account for. I did not cease trying to make schemes for meeting her. It was more difficult than it would ordinarily have been, owing to Tom's still being liable to become suspicious at the hint of anything mysterious. I did not dare to invite her to the house, as I should never be able to explain our acquaintance.

February ended, March began, without our finding a day of meeting.

We then had a translation.

Fairly early in March, Tom's firm gave a party to their employees in order to celebrate young Mr Bendale's coming of age. It was to be a very good party, and was to take place in the Hanover Rooms at the Crawford Hotel. A dinner was to start the proceedings, a short concert would follow, and a dance would end the festival.

I had got a very nice evening dress for the occasion, and Tom bought me a bunch of real flowers to pin on it.

Just as we were arriving at the hotel, I thought of Elizabeth, and the switch occurred, with the usual symptoms. I found myself in the dining room at Heringdon.

About a dozen people, all in day clothes, were sitting round the dining room table. Lord Pottlesham was next to me. Gerald was there, at the opposite end of the table, but all the other people, with the exception of Mrs Farnborough, were strangers.

I was delighted to see Lord Pottlesham again, and listened intently to what he was telling me, which seemed to have a good deal to do with tariffs. I regretted that Tom was not there to hear him.

Lord Pottlesham had evidently failed to notice my temporary giddiness, but a young man with an eye-glass who was sitting at my other side, enquired in a low voice if I was all right. I, a little impatiently, assured him that I was, as I did not want to interrupt the Earl, and added that I had only closed my eyes for a moment, as I had something in them.

"Then you certainly had good reason to close your eyes," said the young man, "I felt quite sure you had." His eyes twinkled, but I turned again to my other neighbour, not to miss the chance of hearing what he had to say. I wondered a little why nobody was in evening clothes, when Gerald and I had dressed for dinner that other time when we were quite alone. Most of the people did not look very smart either. Mrs Farnborough stood out from the company in a smart-looking day dress.

There were more ladies than gentlemen.

I had not been talking to Lord Pottlesham very long when he looked at his watch and asked if we ought not to start; I looked along the table towards Gerald, who seemed to be of the same opinion, saying that Merkleby was some way off.

When we came out of the dining room, I gathered that we were all going to proceed somewhere or other. A business-like woman in spectacles said that of course it was not her business to hurry me, but hadn't I better put on my things.

A bunch of us then went to my bedroom, where I found a lovely sable coat waiting for me. One of the older ladies, who seemed all teeth, talked enthusiastically to me about how wonderful it was to have Lord

Pottlesham coming to speak in Merkleby; what a marvellous meeting it would be, and how clever it was of me to persuade him. Some of the other ladies then cheeped round me like sparrows picking at a lump of bread in snowy weather.

I noticed that they addressed me as Lady Elizabeth, not Lady Forrester. I wondered if this was because they knew Elizabeth well, or because it was the proper thing to call her. I decided to ask her sometime.

Foley, who was buzzing about, gave me a bag and some gloves, and when a discreet knock came at the door, went to answer it. She returned saying that the Major had sent up a message asking was I ready to start. The brood of ladies stopped powdering their noses and putting their hats straight; we all flocked downstairs, where we found the gentlemen in coats and mufflers, and Gerald busy talking to Mrs Farnborough.

Our party then boarded several cars. I found myself in one with Lord Pottlesham, two oldish ladies, one whose coat smelt of camphor, and a thin pale man. Gerald and Mrs Farnborough went together, accompanied by the young man with the eye-glass. We bowled along smoothly through the dark. I had never driven along country roads unlit by lamps before. The night was very dark, but the strong headlights of our car made the road and the hedges look as if they were covered by snow. It was pretty. I could not help admiring aloud. Whereupon Lord Pottlesham talked a great deal about the effects of light and the other three joined in.

I wondered how Elizabeth was getting on. I felt less frightened of her now that we had met, and I knew that she was not my enemy, but a fellow victim. At the same time, I hoped that she would be careful at the Bendale party, and not offend some of Tom's colleagues by failing to recognise them, or, if Mr Bendale spoke to her, which he would be sure to do, be able to laugh at his jokes. I grew nervous at the thought of the harm she might do Tom if she offended his chief. I was divided in my mind between enjoyment of my present adventure, attending a political meeting with a real Cabinet Minister, and regret that I was missing the firm's party, and should not be able to talk it over with Tom afterwards. If only the two things could have happened on different days. I knew Elizabeth would dance better than I could, but would she behave discreetly? She did not seem like a fast woman to talk to, but her standards were different to mine.

The car rolled on, we swished through villages, hedges and trees appearing floodlit for a moment as we passed them, and then magically going back into the dark. Lord Pottlesham was now asking questions about the constituency, which the others were answering. I kept discreetly silent, but I treasured up one or two of the Minister's remarks in order to tell Tom.

At last we reached a little town, which one of my fellow passengers said was Merkleby. It is pronounced 'Markleby,' I discovered later. It was lit by very feeble lamps, and had pavements made of cobblestones, which must, I thought, be uncomfortable to walk on. The car stopped in front of a red brick building, and several men came to meet us, one of them being a Mayor, I heard, though he did not wear his gold chain. We went along a stone passage and into a room with a very flaring light, where there were more people—and I found myself shaking hands with Lord and Lady Rockley.

XXI

A sort of Colonel-looking man with a white moustache shook hands next, and seemed to think that we were a little late. Gerald said something about women and the hours they took tittivating, and the Mayor said that it was worth it when the result was so good, and chuckled and got red. Somebody then suggested that it was time we began, and we went through a door right on to a platform.

I had been to political meetings with Tom, but never sat on the platform before. I felt rather as if I were on the stage with the audience looking at me, and as if all the eyes in the room were fastened on me, which of course was nonsense. There was a good deal of clapping and stamping when we appeared, especially for Lord Pottlesham and the young man with the eye-glass, who was, I discovered before the end of the meeting, Mr Ware, member for the constituency.

The Mayor sat in the middle with Lord Pottlesham on one side of him, behind a table with a bottle of water and glasses on it, and the rest of us sat in rows. The Rockleys and Mr Ware and Gerald and I and the Colonel (he *was* a Colonel by the way) in the front one. Lord Rockley was next to me, and Gerald was between Lady Rockley and Mrs Farnborough. There were a good many speeches. Each speaker said what a privilege it was to have Lord Rockley present to-night. I thought that most of the speakers repeated themselves a good deal, but the audience did not seem to mind.

It was very hot in the room and one or two people had very loose sounding coughs, and once a baby cried and had to be taken out. Lord

Pottlesham spoke beautifully, and said things about the spirit of the Empire that made me wipe my eyes. He went on for some time.

How strange it is that one's thoughts wander sometimes; though I appreciated every word he said, for no reason that I could discover, I thought of Mr Marshall.

Mr Ware spoke next, and said very fine things too, though he made plenty of jokes. During his speech two men interrupted and asked questions. Mr Ware made a joke each time, and everybody laughed and clapped. It was very clever of him, but I could not help feeling that he had not answered what they had asked. However, they retired baffled.

When the important speeches were over, people began proposing votes of thanks. Everybody seemed to get thanked, and made a speech in reply. Gerald had to say a few words in answer to a speech of thanks to him and me for coming, and bringing Lord Pottlesham; when they mentioned me, and people clapped, I smiled and bowed like Mavis Marley in *Royal Hearts*.

Gerald spoke rather badly and seemed shy, which surprised me.

Lord Rockley answered his vote of thanks much better, and quite shortly, and said how pleased he had been to come to Merkleby, where his family had always had so many friends.

When the meeting was over, it appeared that a good many of us were expected to have supper with the Rockleys at Cottesborough, which was only three miles away. It was a lovely standing-up supper. All sorts of cold things to eat, and hot soup being brought by footmen.

I wished I had my own appetite to bring to bear on it; Elizabeth's system was never so hungry as mine, and when I ate what I would naturally have done, it seemed to give her inside a fullish feeling. Lord Rockley asked me what I had thought of the meeting, and I told him how wonderfully I thought Lord Pottlesham had spoken, and how what he had said about the Empire had brought tears to my eyes. I was fairly launched when I noticed that my host was staring hard at me. I stopped short.

"I did not know you were such an enthusiast, Lady Elizabeth," he said.

"Oh, well—one cannot help feeling patriotic at times, can one? One longs to do something to help."

"It was certainly helpful of you to bring Pottlesham," said Lord Rockley. "We could never have hoped for a big gun like that in Merkleby, unless you had brought him."

Our duet was now turned into a trio by the arrival of Mr Ware, who seemed very pleased with himself.

"What good form Potty was in to-night," he said.

"Lady Elizabeth was just expressing her admiration for him," said Rockley.

"He's a wonderful old bird at a meeting. He has an unending supply of the sort of clap-trap that goes down well."

I was shocked. "Mr Ware, you don't mean to tell me that you think the sort of things Lord Pottlesham said in his speech are clap-trap?"

He smiled as though he thought I meant to be amusing. "Quite right, it does not do to say so, does it?" he remarked, lowering his voice.

"Say so! But surely you spoke on the platform to-night as though you agreed with him?"

"I tried to, but I'm afraid I'm not in Potty's class."

I was horrified. "But Mr Ware, don't tell me that you are not sincere!"

He seemed puzzled. "Sincere, how do you mean?"

"What I mean is, that a Member of Parliament who says things he doesn't mean is getting people who trust him to vote for him on false pretences." I spoke earnestly, as I felt.

Mr Ware looked startled and bewildered. Lord Rockley's voice broke in: "Lady Elizabeth, I'm sure you're dying for a cigarette." He passed me a box. I waved it away.

Just then Lady Rockley joined us, much to my relief. She asked if Arthur was looking after us properly, and then went on to tell us that she had heard that the Labour man had had a big meeting at somewhere or other the night before. She added that Labour was getting very strong in some districts (which she mentioned) and feared we should have a fight at the next election.

"I agree with you," said Mr Ware. "Haggins is a very strong candidate."

"Have you ever met him?" she asked.

"Oh, yes, he is a very decent chap, and a good Tory at heart, I'm convinced."

I longed to ask if all Members of Parliament were quite different to what they pretended to be, but thought that perhaps it would be as well not to embarrass Elizabeth with my views.

Soon after this, everybody began to say "good-bye" to the Rockleys, and go. Gerald left Mrs Farnborough for one moment and told me that he had ordered our cars. We moved out of the dining room and spread ourselves about the house. Then an awkward thing happened.

Lord Pottlesham had been nosing about, looking at pictures and things, and suddenly asked me to show him the Ferneley of which I had told him so much. I had not the smallest notion of what he was talking about, and could not help looking vague.

"You know," he reminded me, "the one of Rockley's great-grandfather. Didn't you say it was in the library?"

I guessed that he was talking of a picture. "Oh, yes, but I daresay Lord Rockley would rather show it to you himself."

"He seems occupied at the moment. We would just have time before the cars come round. Here's the library, I suppose."

We went into a room full of bookcases. I might have guessed that it was a library myself. Over the mantelpiece was a painting of a man in a white wig. I thought that it surely must be the great-grandfather. "There it is," I announced in triumphant tones.

He put on his glasses and peered. "That! Really, Elizabeth, you must be dreaming. It was the Ferneley I wanted to see."

"Oh, is that the wrong one?"

"My dear child, what are you thinking about?" He glared at me as if I had meant to offend him. Luckily at that moment Lord Rockley joined us.

"Forrester is looking for you, Lady Elizabeth," he said.

I hailed him, mentally, as a life saver. "Lord Pottlesham wanted to see your picture," I told him.

"Which?"

"I wanted to see your Ferneley, of which Elizabeth has told me." The Earl spoke testily.

"Oh, yes, the Ferneley is over here." He led us to the opposite end of the room, and turned on a light, which enabled us to see a picture of two men standing among dogs, with a horse near one of them. It did not look nearly so like a family portrait as the other one had.

Lord Pottlesham seemed to admire it, however, and Lord Rockley told him the names of the horse and all the dogs, and explained which of the men was his great-grandfather, and which the groom.

"My dear Elizabeth, you are not going to pretend to me that you don't know the difference between a Ferneley and a Kneller?"

"I—I must have been thinking of something else," I volunteered, feeling uncomfortable because I felt sure that Lord Rockley was listening intently.

Luckily we were disturbed by Gerald who announced that the cars were there, and suggested that it was time we left. We went into the hall; on the way Lord Rockley said polite things about my knowledge of pictures, and Gerald said equal civilities about the beautiful pictures that Rockley owned.

"That is a lovely one," said I, pointing to a charming picture of a cat and kittens in the passage. It was so lifelike that I felt it *must* be good.

Lord Rockley laughed. "I'm glad you appreciate my Aunt Ermyntrude's effort," he said, and as the others laughed too, I felt that I must have dropped a brick again.

We said "good-bye" to the Rockleys in the hall, and Lady Rockley hoped that we would soon come to Cottesborough again and have some bridge.

"Oh—but of course you don't play, Lady Elizabeth."

"Elizabeth can, but doesn't," said Gerald. "She played once, electrified everybody, and never touched a card again."

"Like single-speech Hamilton," said Lord Pottlesham, adding, "what made you do it, Elizabeth?"

I answered nervously, "Oh, just because it was Christmas time, I suppose."

"People have done things that nobody believed they could do, under hypnotic control." This, of course, from our host.

"Oh, Arthur, don't begin on those things at this time of night," said his wife.

Gerald again suggested that we ought to go home, and we left. On the way back our car load discussed the meeting and the Rockleys, and praised the beauties of Cottesborough. We dropped one old lady at her house; the other two passengers appeared to be spending the night at Heringdon. My thoughts travelled to Elizabeth. She must be still at the Hanover Rooms. Before the Forrester's car arrived home, we had switched again.

XXII

I found myself putting on my things in the cloak room of the Crawford Hotel. My feet were tired and burning, as if I had used them a good deal during the evening.

Two other women were with me; I knew them both. Their conversation informed me that the party had been a successful one. I ventured to remark that I had thought so too. One of them, Mrs Wix, said with rather a spiteful expression that I, at any rate, must have enjoyed myself.

I wondered what Elizabeth had done. When I was coated and head-scarved, and had put my dancing shoes in their bag, I went out from the cloak room and found Tom waiting in a passage.

I studied his expression anxiously, and thought that he looked a little worried, but not cross.

"Well, Tommy?"

"Oh, there you are Polly."

Strains of music came to my ears.

"Hullo, is the ball still going on?"

"What are you talking about? Of course it is. They'll keep it up for hours yet. But it's late enough for us. Surely you haven't forgotten that the last bus leaves at twelve. We'll have to hurry to catch it."

We actually took a taxi to the place where the bus started. Tom was rather silent. I asked him if he had enjoyed himself.

"In parts," he answered.

"Weren't you pleased with me?" I enquired, apprehensively.

"You surprised me a good deal. I never knew you could jabber away like that, and not be shy. But I got rather cold feet about the Bendales."

"The Bendales?"

"Well, your asking them to tea on Sunday; of course we should have done so before, but you've always funked it."

"To ask—"Words failed me.

The Bendales, the big boss himself. I had never exchanged more than a few words with him, and had only met Mrs Bendale twice, once at a garden party they had given, and once when I had helped her, in a very minor way, at a bazaar.

Elizabeth had rushed me.

"I wondered if they'd accept," said Tom.

"Accept—"I gave a squeak, and pretended I had bitten my tongue.

I felt rather apprehensive.

"Shall we manage all right? They've never been to us before," he said.

"They don't seem to have minded being asked, or they wouldn't have accepted the invitation. They must be coming because they appreciate your work, Tom."

"No doubt you're right, kiddo, but it seems a bit queer somehow. Wix and Holroyd will be ready to eat me."

"Why? Mr Bendale's godfather to one of the Wix children."

"I know. Wix never stops swanking about it, but he thinks himself a bit above me."

"He only thinks he is, Tom. I'm sure Mr Bendale realises that he hasn't got anyone cleverer, or more hard-working in the business."

"H'm, clever, I don't know, hard-working O.K., but some of the others wouldn't thank you, if they heard you, girlie."

I went in a dazed state to bed.

I had gathered that Tom was proud of me. Evidently Elizabeth had been a success. I was not quite sure that I liked that, or enjoyed the fact that it was she who had made the Bendales promise to come and have tea with us on Sunday.

Tom was a little inclined to cavil at my having danced so much, but evidently I had been circumspect and only danced once with each partner. That part was all right, and Elizabeth had done no harm, but what about the Bendale visit?

I was filled with apprehension about that. I decided that Elizabeth, having got me into it, must help me out. Next day I wrote to her at Heringdon and implored her to arrange a meeting between us at once. She replied by telegram that she would meet me at her house at any time in the afternoon of the following day.

Cost what it might, I was determined to see her, and therefore informed Tom that I had shopping to do in the West End. He looked a little doubtful, but raised no objection, and I was in Branksome Square by three o'clock the next day.

I rang the bell with a certain feeling of trepidation, and asked for Lady Elizabeth Forrester.

She was waiting for me and we shook hands.

"How do you do, Lady Forrester, or should I call you 'Lady Elizabeth'?"

"Lady Elizabeth's right, but a little formal, don't you think, considering how intimate we really are, Polly?"

"Oh, do you mean we might get to Christian names?"

"Well, we are certainly the two most intimate women in the world." Her eyes were twinkling.

"It's very kind of you," I said, "but if we ever met in real life, how could we explain how we came to know each other so well?"

"It certainly would take some explaining. Do sit down."

I did.

Then I plumped it out.

"I feel sure you didn't mean to make trouble for me, but I'm a little nervous about that tea with Mr and Mrs Bendale on Sunday. I shan't know what to talk to them about."

"Why not? Mr Bendale is a nice old thing, though I admit his wife is a bit sticky."

"What made you invite them?"

"It seemed so obvious. Mr Bendale is the head of Tom's business, isn't he? We were standing next to each other, and I imagined that I ought to talk to him. By some lucky chance I found out that he is very much interested in old family photograph albums, so I told him about the ones you have."

"What, those books full of old-fashioned pictures of Tom's grandparents and their relations?"

"Yes, they're marvellous. He was most interested in hearing about them, and when his wife joined us, told her about them too. It appears that he has got a good many himself. So I suggested that they should come and see ours—yours I mean—and chose Sunday as a good day, because I knew that your husband would be at home then, and I felt sure that he ought not to miss such a chance of making friends with his boss."

"But, Lady Elizabeth, didn't they think it cheek, your asking them all of a sudden like that?"

"I don't see why. After all you've got the albums, including a very interesting one of pressed wild flowers."

"Oh, that was made by Tom's great aunt, Cecilia. I always meant to throw it away," I said.

"Oh, please don't, it's perfect, with the descriptions of the flowers, with suitable quotations from the major poets, all in the most divine handwriting. You will amuse Mr Bendale with that for hours."

"I couldn't. I should never know what to say. If only we could change places on that day."

Her face got serious.

"Couldn't we try to? Just as an experiment."

"Thinking over our various translations, haven't they always happened when we were simultaneously thinking of each other?"

"Do you think we could manage it deliberately?"

The thought was a new one to me.

"Would it be possible?"

"Why shouldn't we try! Let's fix on a certain hour, and both concentrate on each other like mad."

"And wish each other back again at a certain hour. Do you think it would work?"

"Why not, and if our translations *are* controllable—"

"And if they're not, I shall be left with the Bendales."

"I'm sure you'll have no difficulty in coping with them, and surely their visit will help Tom?"

"Not if I offended them."

"How could you possibly offend them? You've asked them to tea out of pure kindness of heart, and all you've got to do is to look pleased to see them."

"But—our house, our way of living isn't perhaps quite what they've been used to."

"Don't you think they realise that? It's for pleasure they're coming, not to be impressed."

"But if the tea goes wrong, and Gladys isn't up to the mark, Mrs Bendale will be sure to notice."

"Not if you don't look worried; and if she does it will only make her feel that she is luckier than you, which will put her in a good temper. Let her give you some household advice; you needn't take it, but it will please her; it flatters everybody's vanity to be consulted about something. She'll eat out of your hand if she can instruct you on any point."

I stared. "I never thought of that."

"Oh, everybody likes the feeling of being helpful if it doesn't involve real effort," she broke off. "But tell me how Bobby is. I have been longing to know."

I gave her all the children's news. It did feel strange to be hob-nobbing with her like that.

I asked after Gerald. Then she seemed a little less cordial, but told me that he was staying somewhere for some races.

Though something in her manner warned me off asking all sorts of things that I should have loved to know about them both, I could not help enquiring if Mrs Farnborough would be staying where he was.

"I really don't know. It is quite probable." Her voice was uninterested.

A pause.

"Forgive me, Lady Elizabeth, I only ask because, if we change again, I must know how to treat Major Forrester."

"How do you mean?"

"Er—well, I don't quite know how to say it, but it doesn't seem to me as if you and your husband were friendly—as Tom and I are, I mean."

She sat quite still for a moment; the sad lines on her face deepened. Then she said, in a cold voice:

"Gerald and I are quite good friends. He goes his way, I go mine."

"Please don't be angry with me, Lady Elizabeth. I am not of a prying nature, but—things aren't quite the same between you and me as between most people."

"That's true enough." She gave a short laugh. "What do you want to know?"

"Only this,—do you mind about—about Lady Gilray—I mean Lady Giles, and Mrs Farnborough—their running after him, I mean?"

"Why should I mind? Surely a man has a right to choose his own friends." Her tone and expression both implied that she thought I had asked enough, but I did not care, I went on.

"Would he mind if you had friends like that?"

"Of course not. He's not a savage."

"Supposing that you told him that Mr Buschner tried to—to make up to you, for instance."

"Buschner, what do you mean?"

"Well, he's in love with you, isn't he? I found that out at Christmas time."

"Oh, Buschner! He's always busy adoring somebody, but he's a god at the piano, and fun to talk to." Her face unclouded. "Do tell me what you did to Buschner at Christmas, he's never been the same man since."

"Oh,—I suppose I didn't appreciate his music and told him so, and then he—he got very angry, and tried to make love to me, and of course I reminded him that I was a married woman. That you were, it was really."

She laughed suddenly, a gay and beautiful laugh that was delightful. "And you pulled his leg and made him play musical comedy, and snubbed his ardour into the bargain. What a change for him. Polly Wilkinson, you are absolutely perfect."

I was offended because I had a feeling that she was laughing at me.

"Am I? I don't suppose your husband thinks so."

She stopped smiling.

"What do you make of Gerald?" she said, rather as if the question had come from her in spite of herself.

Suddenly I felt shy. "Oh—I don't know. I expect lots of ladies find him attractive."

"I daresay. Do you? You seem to have taken a certain amount of interest in him."

"He is rather interesting, and it didn't seem as if it was really me."

Her smile grew sarcastic.

"If it had been you, Mr Tom might not have approved."

"Oh … you don't think that I—after all he is your husband."

"Quite." A pause … Later she gave another short laugh. "This is an incredible conversation, isn't it? There can never have been another like it."

"That's right," I answered, "but since it is so incredible, you mustn't think me rude if I do ask things that I wouldn't if we had met at a tea party."

"What do you want to know?"

"About you and Major Forrester. Have you quarrelled?"

"Quarrelled? No."

"But you aren't happy together."

"As happy as a good many people are …"

I burst out: "Oh, don't put me off like that. Do you care for him or don't you? Do you mind when he makes up to other ladies?"

"I've told you …"

"Oh, I know, but is that true? He calls you an iceberg."

"He … what?" She began to grow rather white.

"Well, he said it to me, something about remembering how he once thought he'd married a woman, and not an iceberg."

"And you made him remember?"

I wondered how I had ever thought her blue eyes soft; they were like gimlets.

"Oh, no … he was very bitter, that's why I thought …"

"You thought what?"

"That he loved you, and you were cold and spurned him."

"Oh." She seemed surprised for a moment, then she laughed, but gaily again. "That sounds very romantic, dear Mrs Polly. Don't worry about Gerald and me. Let's think about our scientific experiment. If the phenomenon is controllable, we may be able to stop these surprising and inconvenient transformations. Now, about the time, and hour. We ought to have a dress rehearsal to-morrow."

We put our heads together.

XXIII

Elizabeth had lent me her car to go home in, but I got out of it at some little distance from Barling Road, not wanting to provoke questions.

We had arranged an experimental transfer for next morning at ten, when Tom would be safely at the office, and before I took the kids out.

At ten o'clock I concentrated all my mind on Elizabeth at Branksome Square, for about five minutes. At first nothing happened, and then, wonder of wonders, the whirling sensation became violent, and when it stopped I found myself in her morning room.

So we *could* do it at will.

I amused myself by looking at the room, inspecting the books, furniture, etc., and resisted an inclination to explore the whole house, as I felt that it might make me forget the time, ten-fifteen, fixed for our return journey.

I watched the clock, and, when the time was reached, concentrated with all my might on Elizabeth in my house.

Nothing happened.

Five, ten, fifteen minutes, went by.

I began to perspire.

Had we really switched on purpose, or was it just a coincidence?

The return journey was not working as we had planned.

I was wondering what to do next when the telephone rang. I felt obliged to answer it.

A female voice spoke, asking if I had got her letter, and would I be Madame be Brinvilliers in her matinee of "Famous Historical Villains," in May. I said that I had not received the letter, and who was Madame whatever-it-was.

"But you know, darling, the famous poisoner … seventeenth century … such lovely clothes. Such an original idea—it's never been done before. Perhaps, if you don't like the idea of Madame de Brinvilliers, you'd prefer to be another criminal?"

I announced that I would be Edith Thompson or nobody, and rang off.

Again I switched my thoughts to Elizabeth, still unavailingly.

Again the telephone distracted me.

Another feminine voice spoke through it … This one said that she had rung up Heringdon and they had told her that I was in London, and wanted me to dine for a tiny party on the fourteenth, and bring Gerald.

As I had not the smallest notion of what Elizabeth's ideas on the subject would be, I stated that I would have to consult Gerald, who was away.

The voice suggested that I should accept anyhow, and let her know about him later. I got rid of her with some difficulty, and made her promise to write later when I should have seen my husband, and could give a definite answer.

It was now after eleven, the children should have started for their walk.

I concentrated again. This time it worked. I found myself out of doors with Bobby walking beside me, and Betty being pushed by me in the pram.

I had to stand still and let the giddiness pass. Bobby noticed my trouble and seemed anxious, but I reassured him and took the children for the remainder of their walk.

On my return home, I discovered that the man had called about the sink, and Miss McGee, who was getting up a bridge tournament to help clear up the debt on the Church organ. Miss McGee is the kind of person who talks nineteen to the dozen. So it was not wonderful that Elizabeth's thoughts should have been distracted.

This experiment had shown us that we could change over at will. Could we stop being changed at all? I did not particularly want to put an end to our adventure until Sunday was safely over.

When Sunday came Tom was all on the hop, though he pretended to be quite calm. He brushed his hair and settled his tie a dozen times.

Punctually at four o'clock I retreated to my bedroom, and sent my thoughts to Elizabeth. In ten minutes the spell worked, the blessed dizzy feeling manifested itself and, in one whirl, I was safely out of reach of the Bendales, alone in Elizabeth's sitting room at Heringdon.

I heaved a sigh of relief, and determined to keep my thoughts off Elizabeth at all costs, and avoid the chance of an involuntary return to my home, while the guests were still there.

I left the room and went downstairs to see what I could find for distraction. The house seemed deserted. It looked tidy and well-kept, as always. I felt a sudden desire to inspect the kitchen department, and see how the Heringdon servants managed. Naturally, I did not know the way, and decided that I could scarcely dare to ring and ask a menial to conduct me to my own kitchen.

I explored, opening door after door, till I found myself in a passage that did not look as though it led to grand rooms.

At last I opened a door that admitted me to a sort of comfortable looking sitting room, where several ladies were occupied in listening to the wireless and sewing. They all got up when I came in, and looked surprised to see me. I recognised my acquaintance, the cook.

"Oh, good afternoon, Mrs Mellon," I said, remembering what Mrs Forrester had called her. She looked very nice in her afternoon clothes, I thought—better dressed than Aunt Abigail. Someone had turned off the wireless.

I had to find a reason for my being there:

"Oh, Mrs Mellon, I heard that something was wrong with the kitchen range."

"I was not aware of that, my lady." A grand-looking woman joined in. I guessed that was the housekeeper.

"I have heard nothing about it, my lady."

I was losing my nerve, but determined to stand my ground.

"Oh, I thought someone said something … anyway, I'd like to look at it."

Mrs Mellon and her colleague at once prepared to accompany me; I had some difficulty in making one of them go first to show me the way, but I made some joke about the passage floor being unsafe; it was made of stone, and told Mrs Mellon to lead me over it. They both probably thought I was crazy, but we reached our destination.

The kitchen seemed enormous, full of shining pots and pans, and big cupboards. Two girls got up as we came in, and stood shyly in a corner. I wished Gladys and Phoebe had manners like that.

Mrs Mellon did not seem pleased at what I had said about the kitchen range, and showed it to me. A fire was burning in it, which I thought extravagant, and big pots were simmering on it.

I allowed myself to be reassured about the range, and enjoyed myself looking at the room. How astonished Gladys would be if she could see it.

At last, for something to say, I asked the cook how we were provided with stores.

"Mrs Marlow can tell you that, my lady," said Mrs Mellon, stiffly.

"Take me round, Mrs Marlow," said I.

Under her guidance I viewed store cupboards—shelves and shelves with jam and tea and rice, and bottled things. There was enough to stock a shop with. I did not wonder that £1,000 a year seemed little to people who lived like this.

I could see that Mrs Marlow was puzzled by my tour of inspection, but it was too good a chance to miss. So, having expressed myself satisfied with the stores, I asked to see the linen cupboard, giving as a reason that I had not looked at it for some time.

Mrs Marlow escorted me through passages and upstairs and unlocked rooms full of linen, all scented with lavender. I could have spent the afternoon there quite happily, but it was not to be.

The butler came and said that Mrs Farnborough wanted to speak to me on the telephone. Leonora's red-headed successor! I would talk to her all right.

She asked if I could put her up at Heringdon for the night, as she was motoring through to some place the name of which I didn't catch. Before I could stop myself, I heard my voice telling Mrs Farnborough that I was very sorry but was afraid I could not manage it.

"But, darling, why—have you got a very big party? The smallest hole would do for me."

"I'm afraid it isn't convenient," said I, bumping down the receiver.

I felt a little nervous after this, being sure that Elizabeth would not have acted so. I had followed my instinct.

I went into the hall, and found Gerald. He was reading a book and smoking. He got up when he saw me.

"Hullo, Elizabeth, where have you been?"

"Oh—about the house. Mrs Farnborough just rang up."

"Aline? What did she want?"

"She asked if she might come here to-morrow night to stay."

"Ah."

"I said 'No'."

"Good God, why?"

"I didn't want her."

"For any particular reason?"

"This house is not an hotel."

"That's a bit unfriendly, isn't it?"

"Why? I knew she was only coming to make goo-goo eyes at you."

"What the devil—"

"First it was Leonora, now it's this one. I don't think it's nice."

"Elizabeth, have you gone crazy? You started something of this kind before."

"Well, aren't you my husband?"

"Oh, don't be idiotic."

"How would you like it if I carried on with other men?"

"What incredible expressions you use! Where do you get them from? And why the hell do you pretend you care what I do?"

"Why should you think I don't care?"

I was fairly launched on a wave of indignation by now. I knew that my face was flushed, my eyes sparkling.

"You've pretty well showed it to me, haven't you? For ages now you've kept me at arm's length, in spite of occasional cat-and-mouse moments."

"Oh!"

His eyes were blazing.

I paused. I was swimming in very deep waters without a chart. I might get wrecked.

"Isn't that true?" He was scowling now, and there was an angry glow in his eyes.

"Perhaps—" I spoke slowly, choosing my words. "Perhaps we didn't quite understand one another, Gerald. We may have both been making mistakes."

"There didn't seem to be much mistake about it."

"What are you trying to say to me?" His voice was less angry now; he moved towards me.

I wondered if the sympathy I felt for him was inspired by my tenancy of Elizabeth's person, or whether some of it was mine. I did find him attractive.

"I don't know if I can say anything now, Gerald,—it may take time, it's difficult to explain."

"What's difficult to explain?" He came nearer.

"Give me time, Gerald—don't rush at me—try and understand by degrees." That, I thought, could hurt nobody.

He was silent for a moment. I noticed that he was breathing deeply. He spoke:

"You aren't trying to make a fool of me again, are you?"

"No—no—I swear I'm not, but go very slow for a time. I'm sure, I'm certain that—if you try—that—that—"

"That what?"

"That we'll be better friends."

"Do you want to be?"

"I—think I do."

"You think? Why the hesitation?"

"I really can't explain, Gerald. You'll just have to guess, and—don't bother so much about the other women, if you like me best—of course, I don't know that you do."

"Elizabeth, you little fool, don't you know that—"

"Don't tell me!"

I was scared, lest I might hear what she only should be told.

"Not now—if you do—like me, let me see that you do," I said.

"But—"

"Please, please, don't say any more now."

"I'm damned if I understand you!"

"Perhaps I don't altogether understand myself."

That was true enough.

"I'm going now. I really must." I fairly ran up the stairs, wondering agitatedly if I had helped Elizabeth, or not.

He did care for her, whatever he might have done. I was sure of it. And I had a strong instinctive feeling that she loved him. Guiltily, I thought of her marooned in Barling Road, and, before I had time to concentrate, I was home again.

For perhaps the first time in the whole of this remarkable adventure, I returned to my own home and found Tom contented. More, positively beaming. He was walking up and down our sitting room talking happily, when I came back to him. As he was looking in the other direction when I emerged from the usual maelstrom he did not see any of the symptoms of the "coming-to" that I was manifesting on the sofa.

The tea-party had been a success. The Bendales charming. Tom and Mr Bendale had enjoyed a "good crack" together and had understood each other better than they normally had a chance to do in the business-like atmosphere of the office. Tom admired the way I had kept my end up and "taken on the old boy," and was pleased that I had managed to be "so matey" with Mrs Bendale. The children had appeared, and fortunately behaved themselves.

For the first time I blessed one of Elizabeth's visits, though I got a slight shock when I heard, later on, that the Bendales had asked us to dine on a day in the following week.

That was an awe-inspiring prospect. It did not seem to alarm Tom. He was in such a happy temper that even the unexpected arrival of Mr Marshall did not exasperate him as much as those visitations usually did.

Mr Marshall told us that he was on his way to visit a sick friend who lived in our district. He stated that he had dropped in to see us and have a friendly cup of tea. We explained that we had finished tea long ago.

As we had finished tea, he suggested that he should now proceed to visit his invalid acquaintance, and "drop in" on us on his way home, as he knew that to sup alone by his lonely hearth would depress him. Hastily I told him (which was true) that we had asked the Morris couple to come and play bridge that evening, but it failed to put him off. As he did not play, he would talk to whomever might be dummy.

I longed for some of the firmness that had empowered me to refuse Mrs Farnborough's visit to Heringdon, but found myself yielding to force of habit, and allowing him to come.

I decided, however, that we should not be completely victimised by him, and, as soon as he had left, went to the Post Office and rang up Fanny. I told her that I had just remembered that it was the night when

Aunt Abigail had old Mrs Charles to supper (which happened every alternate Sunday), and would she care to come and have a meal with us, and some friends, quietly. She accepted with joy, on condition that Tom called for her, and saw her home, as she knew her mother would not like her to be out alone, late at night. I promised her Tom's escort, but had some difficulty in making him consent when he heard about it. He said that he had not bargained for "old Fanny" as well as "that blighter Marshall." I persuaded him that Fanny, like a lightning conductor, would take the shock of Mr Marshall's presence off us.

"That's all very well, but you said I'd see her home. I don't see the catch of turning-out—leaving a good rubber—perhaps," he protested.

"Nonsense, Tom, Mr Marshall will see her home."

"By George, Aunt Abigail wouldn't like that. She'd never think it proper for Fanny to be taken home by a strange man."

"Tom, if Mr Marshall compromises the girl, he'll have to marry her." Tom exploded with laughter.

"What things you do think of, girlie." But he agreed to fetch Cousin Fanny.

XXIV

The evening passed off very pleasantly. Tom and I played bridge with the Morrises and I discovered that both Mr Marshall and Cousin Fanny played draughts. Luckily there was an old draughtboard in the house, and though two of the men were missing, buttons did duty for them, and Fanny and Mr Marshall were pleasantly occupied for the evening. Cousin Fanny did not altogether approve of cards on Sunday; draughts, chess and spillikins were allowable. Tom said that if you had been to church in the morning, it did not much matter how you amused yourself, in a respectable way, afterwards, as long as you did not make other people work. Mr Marshall was inclined to think this point of view a little continental; he glanced at me when he talked about the dangers of foreign influence on honest English folk, but did not labour the point unduly.

Later in the evening Mr Marshall saw Cousin Fanny home. She bridled and looked very coy when he suggested it, but did not refuse, and I felt that Elizabeth's plans for their future had a good chance of succeeding.

On the following Tuesday I had a letter from Elizabeth saying that she was coming to London, and asked for a meeting between us. As usual this was difficult to arrange, but I was very anxious to see her, and persuade her to take my place at the Bendale's dinner party. I dared not invite her to my house, as her presence there would take such a lot of explaining, and so I suggested that we should meet on Barling Common, where I sometimes took the children on fine days for a treat. Luckily the morning of our appointment was fine, and the children and I took a bus to the Common, and I let them play about.

I found Elizabeth sitting on a seat in the spot where we had settled to meet, smoking a cigarette. I felt friendly towards her, but soon discovered that she felt less amicable about me. She wanted to know what I had said to Gerald.

"Why? Hasn't Major Forrester been nice?" I enquired.

She seemed to find difficulty in answering. Gradually she managed to tell me that he had been charming, but seemed to be expecting more attention from her than usual. I paused for a moment, then summoning up my courage, spoke:

"Lady Elizabeth, I don't want to be inquisitive, or anything like that, but I can't help knowing that there has been trouble between you and your husband. Is it anything you can tell me? Believe me, you can trust me."

She smiled, a funny, twisted, little smile.

"Talking to you is rather like communing with my own thoughts isn't it, sometimes?"

"Perhaps it is rather, but tell me, did you marry him and then find you weren't in love with him? I'm sure he is with you."

She was silent for a moment, looking straight in front of her. "I didn't marry him without being in love with him," she said slowly. Her voice trembled a little.

"Well, then, did he—was there someone who—made mischief between you?"

"It wasn't altogether that. It's difficult for me to talk about it, because I never have, but—it was like this. I believe I told you that I was expecting a baby once?"

"Yes," I said, almost in a whisper.

"There was an accident—I was very ill. I thought Gerald was as sorry as I was, but while I was still ill, he—there was someone—"

"Leonora?" I asked softly.

"No, she came later. Oh! I don't mind his friendships and flirtations, they don't matter, but this—just at that moment when I wanted his affection and his sympathy so much—I had known nothing about it until he had to tell me because the woman's husband was threatening to divorce her. Oh! It came to nothing in the end, the whole thing blew over, he had never meant anything serious, just made a fool of himself, but—somehow—that he could—just then—"

"It was wicked of him!" I cried.

"Oh, no, just foolishness. She was a rotten sort of woman, but attractive, and he lost his head."

"I hope you gave him beans?"

"Beans? What, make scenes? How could I do that? He had told me the whole thing quite frankly, blaming himself for an ass, damning his weakness, telling me how he meant to chuck all that sort of rot for the future. I wasn't angry with him, I had never expected him to be quite faithful, it isn't in his nature, but when he seemed to think that we could, at once, be the same to each other as before—I just—couldn't."

"I should think not indeed. I hope you told him so."

"I couldn't say much. There are things that can't be said, only felt, but I—left it."

"Did you mean to forgive him in the end?"

"It wasn't quite a question of forgiving him. I had had a shock. I wanted a little time to recover. He didn't seem to understand that. Resented it."

"You mean he was angry because you froze him when he wanted to— make up to you?"

She half laughed. "You can put it like that."

"But you never explained to him about the shock, I mean?"

"He ought to have known. I couldn't tell him."

"Did it make you like him less?"

"Oh, no—I only needed—time."

"I see." Then I asked suddenly. "Did Mrs Forrester know?"

"I never told her, but I'm sure she guessed that something was wrong. She was always divine to me, and I felt she was longing for things to come right, and that she loathed Leonora."

"Didn't you?"

"Oh no, one can't loathe Leonora, but she made it difficult for Gerald and me to be frank with each other."

"You mean she got hold of Major Forrester—but why did you let her? I should have given Tom an earful if he had behaved like that to me. Why didn't you put a stop to it?"

"How? Gerald has a perfect right to have his own friends."

"Friends—indeed, it was a jolly good flirtation what I saw of it! But I'm sure he only fell for her because you wouldn't have anything to do with him, just the same as that Mrs Farnborough. He loves you—don't you want him back?"

"It doesn't appeal to me, being one of a mob."

"Oh, you wouldn't be. I'm certain of that. It's you he cares for, even if hussies do run after him. He's only interested in you. Can't you—encourage him a little?"

"You seem to have done that." Her expression grew harder.

"I couldn't help seeing that he finds you attractive," I said rather nervously, and went on, "Would you rather he was indifferent to you?"

She gave a queer little half shaky laugh. "Oh—I suppose not." She paused for a moment, then added: "And you seem to have given him an inkling of that. He's like a man on the verge of proposing, attentive to my every wish."

"Do you mind?"

"I don't know whether to forgive you, or to be furious with you. This new interest he shows, it is created by you. You must be a more vital sort of human being than I am, Polly."

"Oh, nonsense, it's only because I didn't freeze him; it made him hope that you might get interested in him again. That's what I think. He isn't charmed by me in the least. Everything I do and say that is like myself, he finds ever so odd."

She laughed, not very happily.

"Odd ... if you influence him?"

"Oh, but I don't, you know I don't. You try and see—do let yourself be happy. I would so love to think you were." I meant it: she looked me full in the face, and her expression got kinder.

"You're a very good sort, Polly," she said. "Forgive me for calling you Polly, I know that you don't want me to, but I must when we are alone."

Just then the children discovered something that they wanted to show to me, and came running up. They said: "How do you do?" nicely to Elizabeth, and she was charming to them, though I guessed how funny she must be feeling at seeing them shy with her, when she knew them so well.

Bobby, after looking hard at her, said suddenly: "How funny, you've got a look on your face just like mummy has sometimes."

"Perhaps I was thinking some of the same thoughts that mummy does." She smiled and said to me: "Children notice things sometimes as well as dogs do."

After a time the kids left us, and I tried to persuade her to take my place at the Bendales. The idea appeared to amuse her, but the date was inconvenient, as she had people coming to dine with her that night. She ridiculed my fear and urged me to make friends with the Bendales, saying that I really should do so and not be shy, for Tom's sake. She assured me again that they were not difficult to talk to and gave me hints about subjects that interested them both.

I agreed a little reluctantly that perhaps I ought to try and get on with them myself.

She laughed suddenly. "I wonder how many people in this world would jump at a chance to change places with one other, especially on tiresome social occasions. I'm sure that we, personally, are thrilled by each other's bores. For instance, I gather that you are amused by old Potty, while I am charmed by Mr Marshall. We ought to change over for fun on purpose sometimes when there's something doing. That would be better than getting mixed up with each other's private lives at inconvenient moments."

"If we really ever change on purpose," I said.

"Well, we tried, didn't we? And it more or less came off."

"Perhaps we shall get quite perfect at it with practice."

Then she suggested making a compact with me, that, in the event of an involuntary switch, we should arrange to think hard of each other fifteen minutes after it had happened, and that if the first effort was no good, to wait and concentrate again a quarter of an hour later.

"If we both remember to do it together, it may get us out of all sorts of trouble," she said.

I asked why fifteen minutes.

She said that it was a nice easy time to remember, and that the immediate moments following any change were generally too full of bewilderment for concentration.

We then told each other about the interferences that had prevented our mutual concentration on the occasion of our last transmigration.

It was now time for me to take the children back home. She drove us back in the car, not the Rolls Royce that I already knew, but another one.

The children thoroughly enjoyed the ride.

XXV

When the children that evening told Tom about the lady who had spoken to us on the Common and given us a lift home, he had no difficulty in believing that anyone might be charmed by the kiddies, and was not suspicious. He only teased me a little about some more of my "nobby friends."

Things now went pretty smoothly for a time. We had an involuntary translation, when I found myself in a dressmaker's shop being fitted for a dress, and created some concern among the fitting ladies who thought I was going to faint.

Though I was thrilled by being actually inside one of these establishments, and longed to ask for all the dresses to be paraded so that I could look at them, I checked my desires in that direction and the fifteen minutes' arrangement worked. I found myself at home without any difficulty and there were no complications, beyond the startling of Gladys who had come in to consult me about some household matter, and thought I had come over very queer. I explained that it was all caused by indigestion, and as she had an aunt who suffered from stomach trouble complicated by giddy fits, all passed off well.

The Bendale dinner party went off fairly well. It took place in their nice house at Hampstead. There were two other people to meet us.

I was envious of the way in which their parlour-maids waited on us, in a quiet and perfect style, miles beyond the powers of Gladys and Phoebe, in spite of my training of them, but I remembered the footmen at

Heringdon and Thinnesley, and was not overawed. Tom got on very well, but I could not help feeling that I disappointed Mr Bendale a little and did not come up to Elizabeth's standard.

I was more in harmony with Mrs Bendale, who gave me ever so many recipes and much household advice. She seemed to have an impression that I was extravagant. I could understand that, if Elizabeth had been discussing housekeeping with her on the Heringdon basis.

On the way home, Tom, though very pleased with his evening, did remark that I had not had such a success with the old man, as I had had on the day he and his wife came to tea with us. I answered that one was always more confident on one's own ground.

After that, no more switches occurred for some time. On several occasions I tried to think myself into her shoes, without avail. I saw in the paper that she and Major Forrester had been staying with somebody or other in Ireland for fishing.

March turned into April.

The great matter which began to excite our family at this time was the serious courtship of Cousin Fanny by Mr Marshall. He went to see her at Aunt Abigail's, which was a relief to Tom and me. Unfortunately, Aunt Abigail took a dislike to him, and said that she was tired whenever he called, and always needed Fanny particularly on these occasions.

Fanny grew desperate. She came to see me, almost in tears, and though her shyness would not allow her to admit how much she liked him, complained of being deprived of opportunities of talking to an intellectual and improving friend.

I made my house their meeting-ground after that, which did not altogether please Tom. Still, all the world loves a lover, and even Mr Marshall, in that part, was not entirely unsympathetic. Cousin Fanny seemed to grow younger every day.

The family watched with amusement, and helped. Mabel and George asked them to supper and the pictures. Ethel and Syd had them to tea;

Syd even lured them to a concert, which I think they enjoyed as little as the Rumanian play, but they did not mind, as they went together. A good half of these meetings were concealed from Aunt Abigail; Fanny justified the deceit on the grounds that it would be wrong to worry her.

I could not help wondering what the old lady thought of Fanny's sudden popularity with her relatives.

Mr Marshall, though full of praises of that "well brought up Miss Wardrop," was very slow in coming up to the scratch; but the family kept on asking them out and hoped for the best. I believe George and Syd had a bet as to whether Mr Marshall would pop the important question this year or next.

What made everything extra difficult was that Cousin Fanny would never dream of being allowed to go out alone with Mr Marshall, and he would have thought it disrespectful to propose taking her.

One day towards the end of April, Mr Marshall offered to take my kiddies to the Zoo. I jumped at the idea. I knew the children would love it. Tom, though invited, cried off. He said that he did not mind the Zoo, but that in a company including Cousin Fanny and Mr Marshall, he would feel too much like one of the permanent inhabitants. This decision of Tom's made it easier for us to choose a weekday, and so avoid Saturday and common crowds.

We all went in the morning; Cousin Fanny, Mr Marshall, the kids and Milly Hopkins, our eighteen-year-old neighbour, whom the children love. We took her because Bobby had told Mr Marshall that it was her birthday. I must say he is kind, if boring. Mr Marshall did not seem to mind being the only man. He made jokes at lunch, which we had at Spiers and Ponds, and told us all sorts of things about natural history, to which Cousin Fanny listened earnestly, though the children wriggled a little, especially Betty. They wanted to see the animals, rather than hear about them.

After lunch we started on our animal viewing; the children enjoyed it madly and got far less tired than I did. My shoes were rather tight. At last I was obliged to sit and rest, while Milly Hopkins and the children went for a ride on the elephant, and Fanny and Mr Marshall went to gaze at the baboons. I was wondering if it would be respectable behaviour to take off a shoe in public and give my toes a chance to spread themselves out, when I suddenly saw Lord Rockley.

He came quite close to me, looking at some cage or other. I gave a little gasp which drew his attention. He glanced in my direction, looked attentively at me for a moment, then smiled and raised his hat.

"Good afternoon, Mrs Wilkinson." He seemed pleased to see me and asked what had brought me to the Zoo.

I told him that I was here with a family party, and enquired what had brought him. He said that he often came.

He enquired after the children, and after chatting for a moment or so, sat down beside me, like an old friend. I was glad that Tom was not in the neighbourhood.

He asked if I had ever received a letter he had written me, and wanted to know whether I had had any more telepathic experiences.

I said, "No."

If he was disappointed he did not show it, and continued talking away quite cheerfully about all kinds of things.

We laughed over some of the animals and some of the people passing, and then suddenly, about some old gentleman or other, I said:

"Like Lord Pottlesham looking for the Ferneley picture at Cottesborough."

I had been talking to him so naturally and pleasantly that I had quite forgotten the curious double nature of our acquaintance. His startled face brought me to full realisation of what I had done. I blushed scarlet.

"Mrs Wilkinson, you have just said an extraordinary thing," he said slowly.

"Have I?" I could feel that my confusion showed.

"Have you ever been to Cottesborough?"

I was silent and looked down at my feet.

He went on: "Once before now I learnt from you that you spoke of places which you had never visited—of which you knew nothing. I'm not being impertinently curious, but you know how much interested I am in these things. Do tell me if you have some wonderful telepathic power."

"Do you think I have?"

"You have just mentioned an incident which took place a few weeks ago, when I am sure you were not present."

Still I did not answer.

"Do you know Lord Pottlesham?"

I hesitated, could hardly say that I did.

"N—no," I said.

He was silent for a moment, then, "Do you know Lady Elizabeth Forrester?" he asked.

I knew then what people mean when they talk about jumping out of their skins.

"Good Heavens, why?" I gasped.

"In some ways you remind me of her."

I grasped that she had told him nothing. Never would I tell the story either.

I reflected for a moment, then said slowly, "I've seen Lady Elizabeth. Why do I remind you of her?"

"Oh—things you have said—" He stopped short and looked at me, then smiled. "I have a feeling that both of you have this in common; you could each tell me a very interesting story if you wanted to."

He got up and raised his hat. "Good-bye, Mrs Wilkinson, I hope we shall meet again some time."

I decided that if I could help it we never should.

Soon after this the kiddies got tired; and we began to look for Cousin Fanny and Mr Marshall. They took some finding, but we came upon them suddenly, holding hands in front of the chimpanzees.

They let go of each other very quickly when they saw us, and Fanny gurgled something about Mr Marshall helping her to do up her glove. From her blush, and from a certain triumphant expression on his face, I guessed that either George or Syd had won a bet.

XXVI

It was true. Mr Marshall had proposed to Cousin Fanny. There was tremendous excitement in the family.

Of course, Aunt Abigail refused her consent, and when it was pointed out to her that Fanny, at forty-three, could hardly be called a minor, and therefore didn't need it, threatened to die. There were floods of tears from Fanny, and very long sentences from Mr Marshall, whom Aunt Abigail refused to see, as the sight of him brought on her "spasms." I wrote and told Elizabeth all about it. She wrote back and advised me to get the lovers to elope, or suggested that Fanny should die back at Aunt Abigail. Elizabeth was still in Ireland.

About this time I tried to arrange a switch with her, but it failed.

I suggested an elopement to the courting pair, but Mr Marshall did not think such things respectable, and Cousin Fanny swore she could never forgive herself if she killed her poor dear mother.

When Tom heard that, he said she'd deserve a medal, presented to her by public subscription, if she did.

Fanny also refused to feign mortal illness, as it would be deceitful; but did not have to in the end, as she suddenly became so ill from worry, and getting poisoned by something she had eaten, that Aunt Abigail was frightened into health, and only concerned to save her darling child, without whom life would be a blank.

Mr Marshall said there was no need to feel that she was losing a daughter, as she was, on the contrary, gaining a son, and if they all three lived together, nobody need be unhappy. So the clouds rolled away from Fanny's mind, and nothing was spoken of but preparations for the wedding.

All this time I had had no translations, either voluntary or involuntary, with Elizabeth.

She arrived in London at the beginning of May, and I went and lunched with her then, alone at her house. She was looking very well, and quite different somehow. As she talked and smiled, her beautiful face was alive, and I thought that she had been like a lovely unlit lamp in the past, and that the change in her now was that the lamp was alight.

She kissed me when we met, and we had a very gay lunch. She wanted to hear all about Cousin Fanny and Mr Marshall, and laughed a good deal at the idea of their household.

"They really ought to be grateful to you, Elizabeth," I said.

She laughed.

"I don't know if Mr Marshall will be when he's had Aunt Abigail on his hands for a time."

She told me that she and Gerald had enjoyed themselves in Ireland, and caught masses of fish, and that she had longed to send us some, but had not dared to.

She said that, when the servants were out of the room. They only brought in the courses and went away; she rang a little silver bell when she wanted them to come in again.

After lunch we went into another room and talked more seriously. I was very anxious to know why none of our attempted switches had been successful.

"Perhaps there was 'interference,'" she said.

"Interference? Like wireless?" I did not quite follow her.

Her brows met.

"Polly, you and I cannot account for this curious experience of ours, though we've both been puzzling about it. I think that thought is a force which creates vibrations, and through our mutual vibrations we establish a sympathetic contact which—"

"Do put it more plainly, Elizabeth," I said, "or I shall never understand."

"Oh—understand." She made a quick, impatient gesture. "I don't begin to understand; one cannot understand miracles. The best way to treat a miracle is to accept it, I suppose."

"Well, we can't help accepting ours," I stated. "We know it happened, even if we cannot explain why."

"You're quite right," she mused. "I suppose we were so much at one, in our longing to escape from our lives, at the same identical moment, that, by some incomprehensible agency, we were enabled to exchange personalities."

"Oh, not personalities," I cried.

"You're right, Polly, we carried our personalities, feelings and prejudices with us into each other's surroundings." She went on thoughtfully. "I have always wondered how much mentality dominates physique, and how much physical reactions influence mentality; and then there is the nervous system acting as liaison officer between body and mind, transmitting messages from one to the other."

"I wonder if your trained physique would have carried my unaccustomed mentality through the riding episode, if I had dared to trust it," I said.

We both laughed.

"I am afraid you had a rough passage that time, Polly."

"I certainly thought hard things of you for putting me in that mess," I said.

"It would have been horrible if I had," she answered.

"And you made my fingers play the piano. How did that work?"

"Well I had rather to concentrate on the difficult passages."

"It must have been rather like trying to play tennis with a golf club."

She smiled, then went on:

"But there's one terribly interesting thing about this experience of ours.

We know that there is a mind, a body, and a nervous system, but it also seems that there is an ego as well, apart from them all—"

"Oh, a soul you mean—"

"I suppose that's what I do mean; it's never been analysed or located by anyone yet."

"Well, a motor car must have a driver, of course."

"That seems to put it in a nutshell," she laughed. "The cars change drivers."

"But why can't we switch any more now? Why has it all come to an end?"

"Perhaps, as I said, there's been interference." Her eyes looked as though they saw something in the distance.

"Interference?"

"Like atmospherics in wireless, some alteration in the rhythm has interfered with transmission."

She did not speak for a moment, then suddenly asked me to tell her more about the Marshall–Wardrop wedding.

"I should love to come to it," she said.

"Oh, I should like to be there myself!"

"Naturally, I was thinking of an invitation, not a translation."

"Oh, that would never do," I cried hastily.

Her laugh rang out.

"Why the horror, Polly—couldn't we arrange an acquaintance somehow?"

"Well, apart from the explanations, I don't think it would quite do."

I explained. I told her that I did not think that my belongings and her's would mix at all well. In our own real persons we would not fit into each other's surroundings. Besides, the real fun of the situation was the adventure of being in another camp, unknown.

She thought for a moment, then said: "Perhaps you're right, Polly. I believe you're a very wise person. We might not find each other's friends and relations so thrilling if they were just ordinary people we could visit."

"And with whom we shouldn't, in the normal way, have much in common."

"Oh—much in common—" she sighed, "I think every human soul is pretty lonely really."

"But sometimes there are things that one can understand—"

"The fundamental resemblances are more important than the superficial differences? Is that what you mean, Polly?"

"I don't know whether I can take all that in."

I got up.

"I think I should be going now, Elizabeth. The family will be wondering where I have got to. I wonder whether we shall ever switch again?"

"Perhaps." She was standing now, facing me.

I had a feeling as though she wanted to tell me something.

Suddenly she leant forward, put her hands on my shoulders and kissed me lightly on the cheek. "I have things to thank you for, Polly."

I felt that I understood; there was a burning feeling behind my eyes. "Oh, nonsense, Elizabeth, you'd have put everything right in the end, its only that you're reserved—and—and make people think you have no feelings, because you hate showing them."

"Well, it is not the custom to undress one's body in public, so why one's soul?"

"Well, if you hide either too much, how is anyone to recognise you?"

She laughed.

"You are a profound philosopher, Polly."

"Oh—am I? That would surprise the family a bit! But I'm not wise enough to know why these switches of ours have stopped; is it because you are more—contented—in your life?"

She smiled. Her deep blue eyes looked very soft. "Perhaps—you see, Polly, I'm going to have a baby."

This, I suppose, is where our peculiar story ends.

There have been no more strange journeys since. Life has gone on in the ordinary way.

In some ways I am glad. It was disconcerting to be waltzed into another existence, but yet—in spite of alarming moments, the translations had their thrills, and every now and again my thoughts go to Heringdon and its inhabitants, and I wonder if perhaps, some day, I shall feel that queer giddy sensation once more.

~ ~ ~

AFTERWORD

~

There can be few persons who have not wished at one time or another to 'change places' with somebody else. In this first novel, one of the most remarkable that have come into the publishers' hands, Maud Cairnes has produced a story in which such a wish is satisfied.

Polly Wilkinson, an unsophisticated but not unsympathetic suburban housewife, is suddenly translated into the body of the chatelaine of a large country house. The possibilities arising from such a situation are obviously infinite, but Miss Cairnes has not confined herself to the more farcical results of Polly's invasion of an alien world but has dealt with the practical problems resulting from such an interchange.

So read the jacket copy on the first edition of *Strange Journey* when it was published in 1935 as the debut novel of Maud Cairnes – who would only go on to publish one more novel, *The Disappearing Duchess*, in 1939. She wasn't the first to use body swapping as the central motif of a novel, but it certainly hadn't yet become the mainstay of popular culture that it is now. And her predecessors in fiction seemed to have concentrated on people who knew each other – a father and son in F. Anstey's enormously popular 1882 novel *Vice Versa*; and a husband

and wife in Thorne Smith's flippant, frenetic *Turnabout* (1931). Cairnes, instead, took class as her theme and chose two strangers to exchange places.

Polly and Lady Elizabeth are not, of course, at totally opposite ends of the class spectrum. While Polly is shown to be a fish out of water in the grand Heringdon estate, her own home is comfortably suburban in one of the south-eastern garden cities that flourished in the first half of the twentieth century. Like Lady Elizabeth, Polly doesn't need to undertake paid employment. She and her husband Tom have domestic staff, and she even goes to Harrods for 'a special kind of silk I needed for a lining'. Even at the time of their marriage, seven years before the novel begins (when Polly was 21 and Tom 25), the household income is above average at £200 a year. It isn't the £1,100 a year that an upper-class character worries will mean poverty – the equivalent of around £60,000 today – but it is certainly not dire for the period.

The differences between the two women that most puzzle those around them are in habits and hobbies, rather than essentials: one can play the piano, for instance, and the other can play bridge. These could conceivably be reversed without any betrayal of class origins, though Lady Elizabeth's ability to ride a horse and tolerance for hunting are firmer markers of her echelon. Smoking is a slightly different matter: Lady Elizabeth seems to be a habitual smoker, while Polly can't stand it. The number of women who regularly smoked rose swiftly through the 1930s, shaking off to a considerable extent the earlier taboo that it was unladylike to smoke. But this was a change that filtered down through the class system, starting, broadly, with women who were young, urban, upper or upper-middle class, and enjoying some sort of independence. A cigarette (in 1920s advertising, at least) was most likely

~~ ~~ ~~

to accompany a girl with a bob and an up-to-the-moment hemline. By the 1930s, smoking was more widespread but still less likely for a housewife than a Lady – but it is worth noting that Polly is disgusted by the taste of a cigarette rather than by any immoral imputation in the suggestion that she would like one.

> "Have a cigarette?" He offered me his case.
> "No, thanks."
> "Off your smoke?"
> "I suppose so."
> It was strange, but now he mentioned it, I was conscious of a strange sort of hankering for a cigarette; it was as though my body wanted one while my mind did not.

A trickier area is the niceties of language. Those who know Lady Elizabeth are surprised by her 'extraordinary phraseology' when Polly is speaking through her – such as "having a tumble" when she falls off her horse, calling her father "Dad", and asking her husband, "How would you like it if I carried on with other men?" In each instance, a twenty-first-century reader might not notice the *faux pas* Polly makes. Each of the terms had been in use for many decades, or even centuries, but the contemporary reader would be expected to know which were suitable to different classes. Similarly, Polly makes an error when asking a butler to announce her to a room as "Lady Forrester". Cairnes takes for granted that the reader will also recognise Polly's blunder: 'Lady Forrester' would connote that she was the wife of a lord, knight or baronet, or had a title in her own right, whereas 'Lady' is accompanied by the woman's first name if she is the daughter of a duke, marquess or earl. And she is properly Lady Elizabeth, since she uses the title as the daughter of Lord Wantage.

Many of the other incidents that confuse those around the women when they swap places are comic bemusements that could affect any two people trying to adapt quickly to a role they don't have a script for. But even these are telling. While both women offend or disturb by blanking people they ought to recognise, there is something touching in the way Lady Elizabeth devises stories of Scottish estates for Polly's children, and an only-hinted-at sadness on her part that she hasn't been able to share these stories with her own children. Perhaps the most successful moments of exchange, requiring the least pretence, are the scenes we don't see of Lady Elizabeth telling elaborate tales.

Polly and Lady Elizabeth do, of course, eventually meet each other and discover they can be allies rather than enemies. Indeed, a pleasing element of the novel is the sisterly way in which both women use their own strengths to help the other to overcome obstacles in their lives – whether marital or impressing Tom's boss. But we are never given the narrative from Lady Elizabeth's perspective, which is particularly interesting when you know that Cairnes herself had far more in common with Lady Elizabeth than with Polly.

'Maud Cairnes' isn't quite a pseudonym, as both the names are there in the author's own – but she has been selective from Lady Maud Kathleen Cairnes Plantagenet Hastings Curzon-Herrick, more generally known as Lady Kathleen. She was the daughter of Warner Hastings, the 15th Earl of Huntingdon, and added the 'Curzon-Herrick' to her name when she married William Montagu Curzon-Herrick. His family weren't unknown to the public either: his sister Mary was dubbed the 'Queen of Beauty' by the press, and was regularly fêted for her looks. As sharp an observer as Cecil Beaton said: "There is no living beauty who can create more of an effect than she when entering a ballroom or sitting in a box at the opera."

~ ~ ~

Though Lady Kathleen's marriage to Curzon-Herrick in 1916 was given a full-page spread in *The Illustrated London News*, her life wasn't given the same broad attention as her sister-in-law's. Living on the vast Beaumanor Hall estate that her husband had inherited the year before their marriage, Lady Kathleen was used to the crowds of aristocrats, the hierarchies of servants, and the shooting parties that would baffle her heroine.

At the same time, she convinces in her portrait of the humbler home. One of the lenses which Cairnes gives to Polly as a way to express herself is contemporary cinema. As the only place where Polly has previously seen upper-class milieus up close, and perhaps one of the few places where she has seen methods of disguise, she frequently relies on copying the actors of the day. Her interest in cinema and actors is evident from the first page, where she expresses her preference for 'talk dark ones with good features and nice slim figures', one of her particular favourites being Ronald Colman. He found fame as an actor in silent movies, before successfully transitioning to 'talkies', receiving Oscar nominations for his first two sound film roles, *Bulldog Drummond* and *Condemned*, both from 1929. Cairnes doesn't specify which Ronald Colman film Polly is hoping to attend, but his most recent film with a romantic storyline was *The Masquerader* (1933) – in which, aptly enough, the politician hero exchanges places with his doppelganger cousin, albeit not supernaturally.

Later in the novel, Polly 'look[s] up at Elizabeth's husband through my lashes, as Vera Ambrose does in *Money for Jam*', and later still she 'smiled at him with my head on one side, like Vera Ambrose'. Elsewhere, she opts for 'opening my eyes very wide, and trying to look innocent like Marina Moyhala, in *Cherry Lips*', 'smiled and bowed

~ ~ ~

like Mavis Marley in *Royal Hearts*, and asks the butler for a guest's car 'just as I had seen Celia Hooper do in the film, *Worried Wives*'. Unlike Colman, these films and actors were made up by Cairnes, though drawing on common archetypes of the period for cinematic ingenues, aristocrats or vamps. Again, somewhat aptly, *Money for Jam* was actually used as a title for a 1943 film where a racehorse and street vendor's horse are inadvertently exchanged.

Polly's impersonations of these actors are seldom a success, and people appear to be confused or surprised ("You're incredibly ghastly when you put on that coy manner, my dear"). Perhaps this is Cairnes' commentary on how inaccurate the film industry is at reflecting the genuine upper classes (even though Polly uses 'the Talkies' as the best explanation she has for why, in one of Lady Elizabeth's periods of inhabiting Polly's body, she has been speaking to Tom with a 'superior way of talking').

For her part, Polly sees through the pretensions and mores of the class she finds herself among – to the heart of the human relationships there. One of the main threads running through *Strange Journey* is the unhappy marriage of Elizabeth and Gerald, and the various flirtations (and more) that Gerald is engaged in (which are apparently more *déclassé* to mention than to undertake). Polly and Tom already have a seemingly idyllic marriage, so their subplot involves matchmaking between secondary characters and also helping the family professionally. The two women offer each other their skills and abilities in a way that class-bound society would not have allowed. It takes this fantastic transition of the women, or the 'translation' as they call it, to get beyond the unwritten rules of Lady Elizabeth's life and to resurrect the marriage. As the novel closes, the couple has been restored and a baby is on the way. It is perhaps the most fairy-tale-like aspect of the plot – but if you can't incorporate something of the fairy-tale into a body-swap novel, then where can you?

Simon Thomas

Series consultant **Simon Thomas** created the middlebrow blog Stuck in a Book in 2007. He is also the co-host of the popular podcast Tea or Books? Simon has a PhD from Oxford University in Interwar Literature.